SPARKS FLY WITH
THE BILLIONAIRE

SPARKS FLY WITH THE BILLIONAIRE

BY

MARION LENNOX

MILLS
BOON

First published in Great Britain 2013
by Mills & Boon, an imprint of Harlequin (UK) Limited.
Large Print edition 2013
Harlequin (UK) Limited, Eton House,
18-24 Paradise Road, Richmond, Surrey TW9 1SR

© Marion Lennox 2013

ISBN: 978 0 263 23214 1

Harlequin (UK) policy is to use papers that are natural,
renewable and recyclable products and made from
wood grown in sustainable forests. The logging and
manufacturing process conform to the legal environmental
regulations of the country of origin.

Printed and bound in Great Britain
by CPI Antony Rowe, Chippenham, Wiltshire

For Dad,
who took me to the circus.
With thanks to Trish, who sent me back.

CHAPTER ONE

HE WAS HOPING for a manager, someone who knew figures and could discuss bad news in a business-like environment.

What he found was a woman in pink sequins and tiger stripes, talking to a camel.

'I'm looking for Henry Miski,' he called, stepping gingerly across puddles as the girl put down a battered feed bucket and turned her attention from camel to him. A couple of small terriers by her side nosed forward to greet him.

Mathew Bond rarely worked away from the sterile offices of corporate high-flyers. His company financed some of the biggest infrastructure projects in Australia. Venturing into the grounds of Sparkles Circus was an aberration.

Meeting this woman was an aberration.

She was wearing a fairy-floss pink, clinging body-suit—really clinging—with irregular sparkling stripes twining round her body. Her chestnut hair was coiled into a complicated knot. Her dark, kohled eyes were framed by lashes almost two inches long, and her make-up looked a work of art all by itself.

Marring the over-the-top fantasy, however, was the ancient army coat draped over her sparkles, feet encased in heavy, mud-caked boots and a couple of sniffy dogs. Regardless, she was smiling politely, as any corporate director might greet an unexpected visitor. Comfortable in her own position. Polite but wary.

Not expecting to be declared bankrupt?

'Hold on while I feed Pharaoh,' she told him. 'He's had a cough and can't work today, but unless he thinks he's getting special treatment he'll bray for the entire performance. No one will hear a thing for him.' She emptied the bucket into the camel's feed bin and scratched the great beast's ears. Finally satisfied that Pharaoh was happy, she turned her attention to him.

'Sorry about that, but the last thing I want is a camel with his nose out of joint. What can I do for you?'

'I'm here to see Henry Miski,' he repeated.

'Grandpa's not feeling well,' she told him. 'Gran wants him to stay in the van until show time. I'm his granddaughter—Alice, or The Amazing

Mischka, but my friends call me Allie.' She took his hand and shook it with a shake that would have done a man proud. 'Is it important?'

'I'm Mathew Bond,' he said and handed over his card. 'From Bond's Bank.'

'Any relation to James?' She peeped a smile, checking him out from the top down. It was an all-encompassing scrutiny, taking in his height, his bespoke tailored suit, his cashmere overcoat and his classy, if mud-spattered, brogues. 'Or is the resemblance just coincidental? That coat is to die for.'

To say he was taken aback would be an understatement. Matt was six feet two, long, lean and dark, as his father and grandfather had been before him, but his looks were immaterial. Bond's Bank was a big enough mover and shaker to have people recognise him for who he was. No one commented on his appearance—and he had no need to claim relationship to a fictional spy.

Allie was still watching him, assessing him, and he was starting to feel disconcerted. Others should be doing this, he thought, not for the first time. He should have sent the usual repossession team.

But he was doing this as a favour for his Aunt Margot. This whole arrangement had been a favour and it was time it stopped. Bankers didn't throw good money after bad.

'Your grandfather's expecting me,' he told her, trying to be businesslike again. 'I have an appointment at two.'

'But two's show time.' She tugged a gold watch on a chain out from a *very* attractive cleavage and consulted. 'That's in ten minutes. Grandpa would never have made an appointment at show time. And on Sunday?'

'No. Henry said it was the only time he was available. I told you, I'm from the bank.'

'Sorry, so you did.' Her cute pencilled brows furrowed while she watched him. 'Bond's Bank. The bank Grandpa pays the mortgage into? He must be just about up to the final payment. Is that why you're here?'

Mortgage? There was no mortgage. Not as far as he knew. Just a pack of geriatric animals, eating their heads off.

But he wasn't about to discuss a client's business with an outsider. 'This is between me and your grandfather,' he told her.

'Yes, but he's not well,' she said, as if she was explaining something he really should have got the first time round. 'He needs all his energy for the show.' She glanced at her watch again, then wheeled towards a bunch of caravans and headed off with a speed he struggled to keep up with. He was avoiding puddles and she wasn't. She was simply sloshing through, with her dogs prancing in front.

'Isn't this weather ghastly?' she said over her shoulder. 'We had major problems trying to get the big top up last night. Luckily the forecast is great for the next two weeks, and we have most of the crowd in and seated now. Full house. Look, you can have a quick word but if it's more than a word it'll have to wait till later. Here's Grandpa's caravan.' She raised her voice. 'Grandpa?'

She paused and thumped on the screen door of a large and battered van, emblazoned with the Sparkles Circus emblem on the side. Matt could see armchairs through the screen, a television glowing faintly on the far bench—and mounds of sparkles. Cloth and sequins lay everywhere.

'Gran's overhauling our look for next season,' she told him, seeing where he was looking. 'She does colour themes. Next season it's purple.'

'But pink this year?'

'You guessed it,' she said, and hauled her overcoat wide, exposing pink and silver in all its glory. 'I kinda like pink. What do you think?'

'I… It's very nice.'

'There's a compliment to turn a girl's head.' She chuckled and banged some more. 'Grandpa, come on out. It's almost show time and Mathew Bond is here from the bank. If you guys want to talk, you need to schedule another time.'

Silence.

'Grandpa?' Allie pulled the screen wide, starting to look worried—and then she paused.

Henry was coming.

Henry Miski was a big man. Looking closely, Matt could see the telltale signs of age, but they were cleverly disguised.

This was Henry Miski, ringmaster, tall and dignified to suit. He was wearing jet-black trousers with a slash of gold down each side, and a suit coat—tails—in black and gold brocade, so richly embroidered that Mathew could only blink. His silver hair was so thick it seemed almost a mane. His outfit was topped with a black top hat rimmed with gold, and he carried an elegant black and gold cane.

He stepped down from the caravan with a dignity that made Matt automatically step aside. The old man was stiffly upright, a proud monarch of a man. All this Matt saw at first glance. It was only at second glance that he saw fear.

'I don't have time to speak to you now,' Henry told Matt with ponderous dignity. 'Allie, why are you still wearing those disgusting boots? You should be ready. The dogs have got mud on their paws.'

'We have two minutes, Grandpa,' she said, 'and the dogs only need a wipe. You want us to give Mathew a good seat so he can watch the show? You can have your talk afterwards.'

'We'll need to reschedule in a few days' time,' Henry snapped.

But the time for delay was past, Matt decided grimly. A dozen letters from the bank had gone unanswered. Registered letters had been sent so Mathew knew they'd been received. Bond's didn't make loans to businesses this small. It had been an aberration on his grandfather's part, but the loan was growing bigger by the minute. There'd been no payments now for six months.

In normal circumstances the receivers would be doing this—hard men arriving to take possession of what now belonged to the bank. It was only because of Margot that he'd come himself.

'Henry, we need to talk,' he said, gently but firmly. 'You made this appointment time. We've sent registered letters confirming, so this can't be a surprise. I'm here as representative of the bank to tell you officially that we're foreclosing. We have no choice, and neither do you. As of today, this circus is in receivership. You're out of business, Henry, and you need to accept it.'

There was a moment's silence. Deathly silence. Henry stared at him as if he was something he didn't recognise. He heard a gasp from the girl beside him—something that might be a sob of fright—but his eyes were all on the old man. Henry's face was bleaching as he watched.

The ringmaster opened his mouth to speak—and failed.

He put his hand to his chest and he crumpled where he stood.

To Allie's overwhelming relief, her grandpa didn't lose consciousness. Paramedics arrived reassuringly fast, and decided it seemed little more than momentary faintness. But faintness plus a slight fever plus a history of angina were enough to have them decreeing Henry needed hospital. Yes, his pulse had stabilised, but there had been heart pain and he was seventy-six and he needed to go.

Allie's grandmother, Bella, summoned urgently from the ticket booth, was in total agreement.

'You're going, Henry.'

But Henry's distress was obvious. 'The circus...' he stammered. 'The tent's full. All those kids... I'm not letting them down.'

'You're not letting them down.' Allie was badly shaken. Henry and Bella had cared for Allie since her mother left when she was two. She loved them with all her heart, and she wasn't risking Henry's health for anything. 'We'll cope without you,' she told him. 'You always said the circus isn't one single person. It's all of us. Fluffy and Fizz are keeping the audience happy. You go and we'll start properly.'

'You can't have a circus without a ringmaster,' Henry groaned.

He was right. She was struggling to think of a plan, but the truth was she didn't have one.

They could lose an individual act without it being a disaster. Given notice, one of the clowns could step into Henry's shoes, but they were down to two today because Sam had flown up to Queensland to visit his new granddaughter and Fluffy and

Fizz were already costumed, prancing in the ring, warming up the crowd.

'We'll manage,' she said but her head was whirling. Without a ringmaster…

'Without a circus master the circus is nothing,' Henry moaned. 'Get me off this thing and give me back my hat.'

'No.'

'Allie…'

'No,' Allie said more forcibly. 'We'll manage. Maybe I can do the announcing myself.'

But she couldn't. She knew she couldn't. Apart from the fact that a girl in pink sparkles didn't have the same gravitas as her grandfather, she could hardly announce her own acts.

What they needed was a guy. A guy in a suit.

Or… Or… She was clutching at straws here, but a guy in a cashmere coat?

The banker had picked up Henry's hat from the mud. He was standing on the sidelines looking almost as shocked as she was.

He had presence, she thought. He was tall, dark and forceful, he had a lovely deep voice and, in his way, he was almost as imposing as her grandfather. Maybe even more so.

She looked at the hat in his hands—and then she

looked fully at him. Not seeing a banker, but…
something else. 'You're Grandpa's size,' she whispered.

'What?'

'With his jacket and hat…you're perfect.' This
was a lifeline—a slim one, admittedly, but she was
clutching it hard. Maybe they could run the circus
without a ringmaster but it'd be a sad imitation of
what it should be—and Henry would know it and
worry all the way to hospital and beyond.

'He can do it.' She turned back to Henry, stooping over the stretcher, taking his hands. 'Of course
he can. I'll write out the introductions as we go.
The thing's a piece of cake.'

'The banker?' Henry whispered.

'He's already in a suit. All he needs is the trimmings. He's Mathew Bond, a close relative of
James, who does so much scary stuff that ringmaster pales in comparison. He made you collapse
two minutes before show time and he's happy to
make amends. Aren't you, Mathew? Have you ever
seen a circus?'

'What on earth are you talking about?'

'Have you seen a circus?'

'Yes, but…'

'Then you know the drill. Dramatics R Us. *La-*

dies and Gentlemen, announcing the arrival all the way from deepest, darkest, Venezuela, the Amazing Mischka...' Can you do that? Of course you can. Grandpa's coat, hat and cane...a spot of make-up to stop you disappearing under the lights... Surely that's not so scary for a Bond.' She smiled but her insides were jelly. He had to agree. 'Mr Bond, we have a tent full of excited kids. Even a banker wouldn't want them to be turfed out without a show.'

'I'm no circus master,' he snapped.

'You hurt my grandfather,' she snapped back. 'You owe us.'

'I'm sorry, but I owe you nothing and this is none of my business.'

'It is. You said you're foreclosing on the circus.' She was forcing her shocked mind to think this through. 'I have no idea of the rights and wrongs of it, but if you are then it's your circus. Your circus, Mr Bond, with an audience waiting and no ringmaster.'

'I don't get involved with operational affairs.'

'You just did,' she snapped. 'The minute you scared Grandpa. Are you going to do this or am I going to march into the big top right now and announce Bond's Bank have foreclosed and the head of Bond's Bank is kicking everyone out right now?'

'Don't be ridiculous.'

'I'm not being ridiculous,' she said, standing right in front of him and glaring with every ounce of glare she could muster. 'I'm telling you exactly what I'm going to do if you don't help. You caused this; you fix it.'

'I have no idea…'

'You don't have to have an idea,' she said. She'd heard the hesitation in his voice and she knew she had him. No bank would want the sort of publicity she'd just threatened. 'You wear Grandpa's hat and jacket and say what I tell you to say and there's no skill involved at all.'

'Hey,' Henry said weakly from his stretcher and Allie caught herself and conceded a smile. To her grandpa, not to the banker.

'Okay, of course there's skill in being a ringmaster,' she admitted. 'This guy won't be a patch on you, Grandpa, but he's all we have. We'll feed him his lines and keep the circus running. We'll do it, I promise. Off you go to hospital,' she said and she bent and kissed him. 'Mathew Bond and I are off to run the circus.'

'If you agree to my requirements,' Mathew said

in a goaded voice. 'We're foreclosing; you'll accede quietly without a fuss.'

'Fine,' Allie said, just as goaded. 'Anything you like, as long as this afternoon's show goes on.'

How had that happened?

He couldn't think of any circumstances—*any circumstances*—that'd turn him into a ringmaster.

He was about to be a ringmaster.

But in truth the sight of the old man crumpling onto the dirt had shocked him to the core. For a couple of appalling moments he'd thought he was dead.

He shouldn't be here. Calling in debts at such a ground roots level wasn't something he'd done in the past and he wasn't likely to do again.

What had his grandfather been thinking to lend money to these people? Bond's Bank was an illustrious private bank, arranging finance for huge corporations here and abroad. If things got messy, yes, Matt stepped in, but he was accustomed to dealing with corporate high-flyers. Almost always the financial mess had been caused by administrative mismanagement. Occasionally fraud took a hand, but the men and women he dealt with almost always had their private assets protected.

He was therefore not accustomed to old men collapsing into the mud as their world shattered.

Nevertheless, his news had definitely caused the old man to collapse. He watched the ambulance depart with a still protesting Henry and his white-faced wife, and he turned to find he was facing a ball of pink and silver fury.

Seemingly Allie's shock was coalescing into anger.

'He'll be okay,' Allie said through gritted teeth, and he thought her words were as much to reassure herself as they were to reassure him. 'He's had angina before, but he's had a rotten cold and it'll be the two combined. But you…I don't care what bank you come from or what the rights and wrongs are of this absurd story you're telling me, but you tell him two minutes before a performance that you're about to foreclose? Of all the stupid, cruel timing… This has to be a farce. I know Grandpa's finances inside out. We're fine. But meanwhile I have two hundred kids and mums and dads sitting in the big top. I'd like to kick you, but instead I need to get you into costume. Let's go.'

'This is indeed a farce.'

'One you're involved in up to your neck,' she snapped. 'Grandpa's obsessive about his role—

he's written it all down ever since he introduced the camels instead of the ponies last year. You'll have a script and gold-embossed clipboard. We have two minutes to get you dressed and made up and into the ring. We have two hundred kids and parents waiting. Let's get them satisfied and I'll do my kicking later.'

'It'll be me who does the kicking,' he said grimly. 'I'm not used to being pushed around, especially by those who owe my bank money.'

'Fine,' she snapped. 'All out war. But war starts after the show. For now we have a circus to run.'

Which explained why, five minutes later, Mathew Bond, corporate banker, was standing in the middle of the big tent of Sparkles Circus, wearing tails, top hat and gold brocade waistcoat, and intoning in his best—worst?—ringmaster voice…

'*Ladies and gentlemen, welcome to the one, the only, the stupendous, marvellous, exciting, magical once-in-a-lifetime experience that is Sparkles Circus. One hundred and forty years of history, ladies and gentlemen, unfolding before your very eyes. Sit back, but don't relax for a moment. Prepare to be mesmerised.*'

* * *

To his astonishment, once he got over shock and anger, he even found he was enjoying himself.

He did have some grounding. After his parents' death, Matt had spent every summer holiday in Fort Neptune with his beloved Great-Aunt Margot. Margot was the great-aunt of every child's dreams. Her sweetheart had died in the war and she'd refused to think of replacing him, but it didn't stop her enjoying life. She owned a cute cottage on the waterfront and a tiny dinghy she kept moored in the harbour, and she always had a dog at her heels. She'd been a schoolteacher, but in summer school had been out for both of them. Child and great-aunt and dog had fished, explored the bay, swum and soaked up the beach.

He'd loved it. In this tiny seaside town where no one knew him, he was free of the high standards expected of the heir to the Bond Banking dynasty. He could be a kid—and at the end of every summer holiday Margot had taken him to Sparkles Circus as a goodbye treat.

Margot always managed to get front row seats. He remembered eating popcorn and hot dogs, getting his clothes messy and no one cared, watching in awe as spangly ladies flew overhead, as men ate fire, as tightrope walkers performed the impossible, as clowns tumbled and as elephants made their stately way around the ring.

There were no elephants now—or lions or any other wild animals, for that matter. That was at the heart of the circus's problems, he thought—but now wasn't the time to think about finance.

Now was the time to concentrate on the clipboard Allie had handed him.

'Here it is, word for word, and if you could ham it up for us, we'd be grateful.'

The look she'd cast him was anything but grateful, but two hundred mums and dads and kids were looking at him as if he *was* the ringmaster—and a man had to do what a man had to do.

He was standing to the side of the ring now, still on show as the ringmaster was expected to be, as he watched Bernardo the Breathtaking walk on stilts along a rather high tightrope.

It had seemed higher when he was a kid, he thought, and there hadn't been a safety net underneath—or maybe there had, he just hadn't noticed.

Bernardo was good. Very good. He was juggling as he was balancing. Once he faltered and dropped one of his juggling sticks. A ringmaster would fetch it, Matt thought, so he strode out and retrieved it, then stood underneath Bernardo, waited for his imperceptible nod, then tossed it up to him. When Bernardo caught it and went on seamlessly juggling he felt inordinately pleased with himself.

He glanced into the wings and saw a lady in pink sequins relax imperceptibly. She gave him a faint smile and a thumbs-up, but he could tell the smile was forced.

She was doing what was needed to get through this show, he thought, but that faint smile signalled more confrontation to come.

Did she really not know her grandparents' financial position? Was she living in a dream world?

Bernardo the Breathtaking was finished, tossing his juggling sticks down to one of the clowns who Matt realised were the fill-in acts, the links between one act and another. Fluffy and Fizz. They were good, he thought, but not great. A bit long in the tooth? They fell and tumbled and did mock acrobatics, but at a guess they were in their sixties or even older and it showed.

Even Bernardo the Breathtaking was looking a little bit faded.

But then...

'Ladies and gentlemen...' He couldn't believe

he was doing this, intoning the words with all the theatrical flourish the child Mathew had obviously noted and memorised. 'Here she is, all the way from deepest, darkest Venezuela, the woman who now will amaze us with her uncanny, incredible, awesome...' how many adjectives did this script run to? '...the one, the only, the fabulous Miss Mischka Veronuschka...'

And she was in the ring. Allie.

Her act included three ponies, two camels and two dogs. The animals were putty in her hands. The dogs were identical Jack Russell terriers, non-descript, ordinary, but with tricks that turned them into the extraordinary. She flitted among her animals—her pets, he thought, for there was no hint of coercion here. She was a pink and gold butterfly, whispering into ears, touching noses, smiling and praising, and, he thought, they'd do anything for her.

He understood why. The audience was mesmerised, and so was he.

She had the camels lying down, the ponies jumping over the camels, the dogs jumping over the ponies, and then the dogs were riding the ponies as the ponies jumped the camels. The dogs' tails were wagging like rotor blades and their excitement was infectious.

Allie rode one of the camels while the ponies weaved in and out of the camels' legs, and the little dogs weaved through and through the ponies' legs. The dogs practically beamed as they followed her every whispered command.

Matt thought of stories of old, of animal cruelty in circuses, and he looked at these bouncing dogs, the camels benignly following instructions as if they were doing Allie a personal favour, at the ponies prancing around the dogs—and he looked at the girl who knew them from the inside out and he thought…he thought…

He thought suddenly that he'd better think nothing.

This was a lady in pink spangles. She was the granddaughter of a client. Where were his thoughts taking him? Wherever, they'd better get back where they belonged right now.

He didn't get involved. Not personally. The appalling sudden deaths of his parents and his sister had smashed something inside him so deep, so huge, that he'd spent the rest of his life forming armour against ever feeling that sort of hurt again.

He'd looked at Allie's face as she'd seen her

grandfather collapse and he'd seen a glimpse of that hurt. It should be reinforcing that armour, yet here he was, looking at a girl in pink spangles…

And then, thankfully, she was gone. The clowns swooped in again, making a game of the pan and shovel they needed—the camels were clearly not house trained—and the show was ready to move on.

He needed to focus on his next introduction.

'Ladies and Gentlemen…' he said, and the circus proceeded.

Interval.

Since when did standing in a circus ring make you sweat? He felt wiped. He headed out through the pink and gold curtains—and was struck by the sheer incongruity of the difference between front and behind the curtains.

The ring was all gold and glitter—a fantasy. Back here was industry. Men and women were half in and out of costumes, hauling steel rods and ropes and shackles, lining up equipment so it could be carried out neatly as needed.

Allie was back in her boots again, heaving like the best of the men. She had a denim jacket over her sequins.

'Time for you to change, Allie, love,' a very large lady yelled. 'Fizz's selling popcorn instead of Bella. We're cool. Allie, dressing room, now.'

'Someone give Mathew the words for the next half,' Allie yelled and shoved the last iron bar into place and disappeared.

He watched her go and he felt the slight change in atmosphere among the women and men behind the scenes.

She was the boss, he thought.

Henry was the boss.

Henry was seventy-six years old.

Matt had thought he was coming to deal with an elderly ringmaster, to tell him it was time to close down. It seemed, however, that now he'd be dealing with Allie, and something told him dealing with Allie would be a very different proposition altogether.

He pretty much had things down pat by the second half.

He introduced acts. He was also there as general pick-up guy—and also…set-up guy for the clowns?

'The gag's on page three of the cheat sheet,' Fizz had growled at him at half-time. 'Henry sets it up for us so you'll need to do it. It'll be weird you reading it but it's the best we can do.'

Right now the Exotic Yan Yan—Jenny Higgs, wife of Bernardo, or Bernie Higgs, according to the staff sheet he'd read '...*fresh from the wilds of the remotest parts of Tukanizstan*'—was there such a place?—was doing impossible things with her body. She was bending over backwards—like really backwards. Her head was touching her heels! Matt was appalled and fascinated—and for some weird reason he was thinking he was glad it wasn't Allie doing the contorting.

He glanced ahead at the feed lines for the gag and thought…he could do this better if he stopped looking at the Exotic Yan Yan.

And he could do this better if he stopped thinking about Allie?

Do it. He read it twice, three times and he had it.

Yan Yan unknotted and disappeared to thunderous applause. Out came the clowns. It was time to take centre stage himself.

Deep breath. Remember the first line.

'Fluffy, I have a present for you,' he called in a *Here Kitty, nice Kitty* voice, and set the clipboard down, preparing—against all odds—to play the ham. 'It's your birthday, Fluffy, and I've bought you a lovely big cannon.'

'A cannon?' Fluffy squeaked, somersaulting with astonishment.

The clowns responded with practised gusto and foolishness as the great fake cannon was wheeled in. The joke went seamlessly, water went everywhere and the audience roared their appreciation.

Exit stage left, two dripping clowns with cannon.

Matt headed back to the sidelines for his clipboard as the ropes and pulleys and shackles were heading out at a run.

Allie, dressed now in brilliant hot pink, with her trademark tiger stripes making her look spectacular, was in the wings and she was staring at him with incredulity.

'You memorised it?'

'I had time.'

'You had two minutes.'

'Plenty of time,' he said and felt a little smug. Banker Makes Good. He motioned to the bars, ropes, pulleys and shackles, set up in well drilled order. 'Let's get this show moving.' He picked up his clipboard and strode out again.

And then Allie was flying in from the outer, twisting and clinging to a rope that looked like the sort of rope you'd hang over a river. She swung to the middle, seized another rope, changed direction—and swung herself up to a bar far up in the high reaches of the big top.

There was a guy up there waiting, steadying her.

It was his turn again.

'Ladies and gentlemen, hold onto your hats. From the wilds of outer Mongolia, from the great, wild warrior hunting grounds of the Eastern nations, ladies and gentlemen, the great Valentino, to be catcher for our very own Mischka. Watch with bated breath while Mischka places life and limb in his hands and see if he lets her down.'

He didn't let her down.

Mathew had watched this act when he was six years old and he'd been convinced the spangly lady would fall at any moment. In fact he'd remembered hiding under his seat, peeping through his hands, afraid to come out until the gorgeous creature flying through the air was safely on the ground.

He didn't watch with quite the same sense of dread now. For a start, he'd seen how big, quiet and competent 'Valentino'—alias Greg—was. He was six feet eight at least, and pure muscle. He hung upside down and swung back and forth, steady and unfaltering, as Allie somersaulted and dived.

Terrifying or not, it was an awesome act.

And Allie…Mischka…was stunning. *She was gorgeous.*

He wasn't the only one who thought so. Matt had fallen in love with the circus when he was six years old. Now he was watching other children, other six-year-olds, falling in love in exactly the same way.

He was foreclosing. He was declaring these people bankrupt. He was putting Mischka out of a job and he was making this circus disappear.

It's business, he told himself harshly. What has to be done, has to be done.

Right after the show.

Now.

For the circus was over. Clowns, acrobats, all the circus crew, were tumbling out to form a circle in the ring, holding hands, bowing.

Allie took his hand and dragged him into line with the rest of them. She was bowing and forcing him to do the same. She was smiling and smiling as the kids went wild and Mathew smiled with her—and for a weird, complex moment he felt as if he'd run away with the circus and he was part of it.

Part of them.

But then the performers backed out of the ring

with practised ease. The curtain fell into place and Allie turned to face him, and all the pretence of the circus was stripped away. She looked raw, frightened—and very, very angry.

The other performers were clapping him on the back, saying 'Well done', grinning at him as if he was a lifesaver.

He wasn't.

The team dispersed and he was left with Allie.

'I suppose I should say thank you,' she said in a tone that said thank you was the furthest thing from her mind.

'You don't need to.'

'I don't, do I?' She was no longer Mischka. She'd reverted to someone else entirely. Even the brilliant make-up couldn't stop her looking frightened. 'But how can I? The rest of the team think Grandpa's sick and you stepped in to save us. They're grateful. Grateful! Ha. To threaten him with bankruptcy.… Of all the stupid… If Grandpa dies…'

She stopped on an angry sob.

'The paramedics said it was only a faint.'

'So they did,' she managed. 'So why should I worry? But I'm worrying, Mr Bond, and not just about Grandpa's heart. How dare you threaten our circus? Give me one good reason.'

There was no easy way to do this. By rights, this was between Bond's Bank and Henry, but Henry was in hospital and this girl had proved conclusively that she was fundamental to the running of Sparkles Circus. More, she was Henry's granddaughter.

She had a right to know.

He had the file in his car, but he hadn't brought it in with him. He'd thought he'd come quietly and put the facts to Henry, facts Henry must already know. But he had a summary.

He reached into his back pocket and tugged out a neatly folded slip of paper, unfolded it and handed it over.

'This is your grandfather's financial position with Bond's Bank,' he told her. 'The balances for the last ten years are on the right. We've been as patient as we can, but no capital's been paid off for three years, and six months ago even the interest payments stopped. The circus's major creditor is winding up his business and is calling in what he's owed. We can't and won't lend any more, and I'm sorry but the bank has no choice but to foreclose.'

She read it.

It made not one whit of sense.

She'd done financial training. One thing Henry and Bella had insisted on was that she get herself professional qualifications, so that she had a fall-back position. *'In case you ever want to leave the circus. In case you want to stay in one place and settle.'*

They'd said it almost as a joke, as if staying in the same place was something bred out of the Miski family generations ago, but they'd still insisted, so in the quiet times of the circus, during the winter lay-off and the nights where there weren't performances, she'd studied accountancy online.

It'll be useful, she'd told herself, and already she thought it was. Henry left most of the bookkeeping to her. She therefore knew the circus's financial position from the inside out. She didn't need this piece of paper.

And it didn't correlate.

She stared at the figures and they jumbled before her. The bottom line. The great bold bottom line that had her thinking she might just join Henry in his ambulance.

It didn't help that Mathew was watching her, impassive, a banker, a judge and jury all in one, and maybe he'd already decided on the verdict.

Enough.

'Look, I need to contact the hospital,' she told him, thrusting the sheet back at him, then hauling the tie from her hair to let loose a mass of chestnut curls around her shoulders. She had a stabbing pain behind her eyes. The shock of seeing Grandpa collapse was still before her. These figures… She couldn't focus on these figures that made no sense at all.

'Of course,' Mathew said quietly. 'Would you like me to come back tomorrow?'

'No.' She stared blindly ahead. 'No, I need to sort this. It's stupid. Go back to Grandpa's van. It's not locked. I'll ring the hospital, then come and find you—as long as everything's okay.'

Mathew dealt with corporate high-flyers and usually they came to him. His office was the biggest in the Bond Bank tower. It had a view of the Sydney Opera House, of the Sydney Harbour Bridge, of the whole of Sydney Harbour.

Allie was expecting him to sit in a shabby caravan among mounds of sequins and calmly wait?

But Allie's face was bleached under her make-up. With her hair let down, she suddenly seemed even less under control. The pink and silver sparkle, the kohl, the crazy lashes seemed nothing but a façade, no disguise for a very frightened woman.

Her grandpa was ill. Her world was about to come crashing down—as his had crashed all those years ago?

Not as bad, he thought, but still bad.

So...the least he could do was take off this crazy outer jacket, fetch the file from the car, turn back into a banker but give her time to do what she must.

'Take as long as you need,' he said. 'I'll wait.'

'Thank you very much,' she said bitterly. 'I don't think.'

'The doctor says he's sure he'll be okay.'

Allie's grandmother, Bella, sounded tremulous on the other end of the phone, but she didn't sound terrified, and Allie let out breath she didn't know she'd been holding. 'Did the circus go on?' Bella asked.

'Yes.'

'Without Henry?'

'We used the banker.'

There was a moment's silence and then, astoundingly, a chuckle. 'Oh, Allie, you could talk anyone round your little finger. See if you can talk him into lending us more money, will you, love?'

Allie was silent at that. She thought of the figures. She thought…what? Why did they need to borrow?

'Gran…'

'I have to go, dear,' Bella said hurriedly. 'The nurse is bringing us both a cup of tea. The doctor says your grandpa should stay here for a few days, though. He says he's run down. He hasn't been eating. I wonder if that's because he knew the banker was coming?'

'Gran…'

'I gotta go, love. Just get an extension to the loan. It can't be too hard. Banks have trillions. They can't begrudge us a few thousand or so, surely. Bat your eyelids, Allie love, and twist him into helping us.'

And she was gone—and Allie was left staring at her phone thinking…thinking…

Mathew Bond was waiting for her in Grandpa's caravan.

Twist him how?

Twist him why?

CHAPTER TWO

SHE CHANGED BEFORE she went to meet him. For some reason it seemed important to get rid of the spangles and lashes and make-up. She thought for a weird moment of putting on the neat grey suit she kept for solemn occasions, but in fact there'd only ever been one 'solemn' occasion. When Valentino's mother died, Valentino—or Greg—had asked them all to come to the funeral in 'nice, sober colours' as a mark of respect.

Allie looked at the suit now. She lifted it from her tiny wardrobe—but then she put it back.

She could never compete with that cashmere coat. If she couldn't meet him on his terms, she'd meet him on her own.

She tugged on old jeans and an oversized water proof jacket, scrubbed her face clean, tied her hair back with a scrap of red sparkle—okay, she could never completely escape sparkle, and nor would she want to—and headed off to face him.

He was sitting at her grandparents' table. He'd made two mugs of tea.

He looked…incongruous. At home. Gorgeous?

He'd taken off his ringmaster coat but he hadn't put his own coat back on. Her grandparents' van was always overheated and he'd worked hard for the last three hours. He had the top couple of buttons of his shirt undone and his sleeves rolled up. He looked dark and smooth and…breathtaking?

A girl could almost be excused for turning tail and running, she thought. This guy was threatening her livelihood. Dangerous didn't begin to describe the warning signs flashing in her head right now.

But she couldn't turn and run.

Pull up those big girl panties and forget about breathtaking, she told herself firmly, and she swung open the screen door with a bang, as if she meant business.

'Milk?' he said, as if she was an expected guest. 'Sugar?'

She glared at him and swiped the milk and poured her own. She took a bit longer than she needed, putting the milk back in the fridge while she got her face in order.

She *would* be businesslike.

She slid onto the seat opposite him, pushed away a pile of purple sequins, cradled her tea—how did he guess how much she needed it?—and finally she faced him.

'Show me the figures,' she said, and he pushed the file across the table to her, then went back to drinking tea. He was watching the guys packing up through the screen doors. The camels—Caesar and Cleopatra—were being led back to the camel enclosure. He appeared to find them fascinating.

Like the figures. Fascinating didn't begin to describe them.

He had them all in the file he'd handed her. Profit and loss for the last ten years, expenses, tax statements—this was a summary of the financial position of the entire circus.

She recognised every set of figures except one.

'These payments are mortgage payments,' she said at last. 'They're paying off Gran and Grandpa's retirement house. There's no way the loan's that big.'

'I don't know anything about a house,' he said. 'But the loan is that big.'

'That's monstrous.'

'Which is why we're foreclosing.'

'You can just…I don't know…' She pushed a

wisp of hair from her eyes. 'Repossess the house? But there must be some mistake.'

'Where's the house?'

She stared across the table in astonishment. 'What are you talking about?'

'The house you're talking of,' he said gently. 'The house that matches this mortgage you seem to think exists. Is it in Fort Neptune?'

'Yes,' she said blankly. 'It's a street back from the harbour. It's small but it's perfect.'

'Have you ever been inside?'

'It's rented. Gran and Grandpa bought it ten years ago. It's for when they need to leave the circus.'

'Have you ever seen the deeds?'

'I... No.'

'So all you've seen is the outside?'

She felt...winded. 'I...yes,' she managed. 'They bought it while I was away and it's been rented out since.' She was thinking furiously. She would have been, what, seventeen or eighteen when they'd bought it? It was just after that awful fuss about the elephants...

The elephants...Maisie and Minnie. Two lumbering, gentle Asian elephants she'd known and loved from the moment she could first remember.

Elephants.

House.

'They sold the elephants,' she whispered, but already she was seeing the chasm where a house should be but maybe elephants were instead.

'There's not a big market for second hand circus elephants,' Mathew said, still gently, but his words were calmly sure. 'Or lions. Or monkeys, for that matter.'

'Grandpa said he sold them to an open-range zoo.'

'Maybe your grandpa wanted to keep you happy.'

She stared at him—and then she snatched up the paper and stared at it as if it was an unexploded bomb, while Mathew Bond's words washed around her.

'Bond's Bank—meaning my grandfather—was approached ten years ago,' he told her as she kept staring. 'We were asked to set up a loan to provide for the care of two elephants, three lions and five monkeys. A wildlife refuge west of Sydney provides such care, but, as you can imagine, it's not cheap. Elephants live up to seventy years. Lions twenty. Monkeys up to forty. You've lost one lion, Zelda, last year, and two of the monkeys have died. The rest of the tribe are in rude health and eating their heads off. The loan was worked out based on costs for ten years but those costs have escalated. You've now reached the stage where the interest due is almost as much as the loan itself. Henry's way overdue in payments and the refuge is calling in its overdue bills. They're winding down. Your grandfather's seventy-six, Allie. There's no way he can repay this loan. It's time to fold the tent and give it away.'

Silence.

She was staring blindly at Mathew now, but she wasn't seeing him. Instead she was seeing elephants. She'd watched them perform as a child, she'd learned to work with them and she'd loved them. Then, as a teenager she'd started seeing the bigger picture. She'd started seeing the conditions they lived in for what they were, and she'd railed against them.

She remembered the fights.

'Grandpa, I know we've always had wild animals. You've lived with them since you were a kid, too, but it's not right. Even though we do the best we can for them, they shouldn't live like this. They need to be somewhere they can roam. Grandpa, please...'

As she'd got older, full of adolescent certainty, she'd laid down her ultimatum.

'I can't live with you if we keep dragging them from place to place. The camels and dogs and ponies are fine—they've been domestic for generations and we can give them decent exercise and care. But not the others. Grandpa, you have to do something.'

'The circus will lose money...' That was her grandfather, fighting a losing battle.

'Isn't it better to lose money than to be cruel?'

She remembered the fights, the tantrums, the sulky silences—and then she'd come home from one of her brief visits to her mother and they'd gone.

'We've sent them to a zoo in Western Australia,' Gran had told her, and shown her pictures of a gorgeous open range zoo.

Then, later—how much later?—they'd shown her pictures of a house. Her mind was racing. That was right about the time she was starting to study bookkeeping. Right about the time Henry was starting to let her keep the books.

'The house...' she whispered but she was already accepting the house was a lie.

'If they've been showing you the books, maybe

the house is a smokescreen. I'm sorry, Allie, but there is no house.'

Her world was shifting. There was nothing to hold on to.

Mathew's voice was implacable. This was a banker, here on business. She stared again at that bottom line. He was calling in a loan she had no hope of paying.

No house.

The ramifications were appalling.

She wanted this man to go away. She wanted to retreat to her caravan and hug her dogs. She wanted to pour herself something stronger than tea and think.

Think the unthinkable?

Panic was crowding in from all sides. Outside, the circus crew was packing up for the night—men and women who depended on this circus for a livelihood. Most of them had done so all their lives.

'What...what security did he use for the loan?' she whispered.

'The circus itself,' Mathew told her.

'We're not worth...'

'You are worth quite a bit. You've been running the same schedule for over a hundred years. You have council land booked annually in the best places at the best times. Another circus will pay for those slots.'

'You mean Carvers,' she said incredulously. 'Ron Carver has been trying to get his hands on our sites for years. You want us to give them to him?'

'I don't see you have a choice.'

'But it doesn't make sense. Why?' she demanded, trying desperately to shove her distress to the background. 'Why did Bond's ever agree to such a crazy loan? If this is true…You must have known we'd never have the collateral to pay this back?'

'My Great-Aunt Margot,' he said, and he paused, as if he didn't quite know where to go with this.

'Margot?'

'Margot Bond,' he said. 'Do you know her?'

She did. Everyone knew Margot. She'd had a front row seat for years, always present on the first and last night the circus was in Fort Neptune. She arrived immaculately dressed, older but seemingly more dignified with every year, and every year her grandparents greeted her with delight.

She hadn't been here this year, and Allie had missed her.

'My grandfather and Margot were brought to Sparkles as children,' Mathew told her. 'Later,

Margot brought my father, and then me in my turn. When your grandfather couldn't find anyone to fund the loan, in desperation he asked Margot. He knew she was connected to Bond's. When Margot asked my grandfather—her brother—he couldn't say no. Very few people can say no to Margot.'

He hesitated then, as if he didn't want to go on, and the words he finally came out with sounded forced. 'Margot's dying,' he said bleakly. 'That's why I'm in Fort Neptune. We could have fore-closed from a distance but, seeing I'm here, I de-cided to do it in person.'

'Because now she's dying you don't need to make her happy any more?'

Her tea slopped as she said it, and she gasped. She stood up and stepped away from the table, staring at the spilled tea. 'Sorry. That…that was dreadful of me—and unfair. I'm very sorry Mar-got's dying, and of course it's your money and you have every right to call it in. But…right now?'

'You've been sent notices for months, Allie. Contrary to what you think, this is not a surprise. Henry knows it. This is the end. I have authority to take control.'

She nodded, choked on a sob, swiped away a tear—*she would not cry*—and managed to gain composure. Of a sort. 'Right,' she managed. 'But there's nothing you can do tonight. Not now.'

'I can...'

'You can't,' she snapped. 'You can do nothing. Otherwise I'll go straight to the local paper and to-morrow's headlines will be Bond's Bank foreclos-ing on ancient circus while its almost-as-ancient ringmaster fights for his life in the local hospital.'

'That's not fair.'

'Fair,' she said savagely. 'You don't know what fair looks like. I haven't even started. Now, I'm going to the hospital to see how Grandpa really is. Meanwhile, you need to get off circus land.'

'Are you threatening me?'

'Yes,' she said, and suddenly the emotion, the anger, the distress built up and she could no longer contain it. 'Now. If I so much as see you skulk-ing...'

'I do not skulk...'

'Or any of your heavies...'

'I don't have heavies.'

'I'll call the police.'

'I have the right...'

'You have no rights at all,' she yelled, and she'd really lost it but right now she didn't care. 'The moral high ground is mine and I'm taking it. Get off circus land, Mathew Bond. I'll sort this mess, somehow, some way, but meanwhile I have my grandfather in hospital, I have a circus to tend and you have no place here.'

She grabbed his half-full mug and her spilled one and she thumped them both into the sink so hard one broke.

She stared at the shattered remains and her face crumpled.

'Well, that's one thing you won't be able to re-possess,' she said at last, drearily, temper fading, knowing she was facing inevitable defeat.

Enough. She stalked out of the caravan and thumped the door closed behind her.

Business shouldn't be personal, Matt thought bleakly. He didn't do personal, and he didn't cope with emotion. It had been a huge mistake to come here himself. He should have sent his trained, im-personal staff who'd do what had to be done and get out of here.

That was what he had to do now, he told him-self. Do what had to be done and get out of here.

So he did.

He filed his papers together, making sure every page was in order and the file was complete. He rolled down his sleeves, he buttoned his shirt and he put back on his grey silk tie.

He put on his cashmere coat and walked out of the caravan, out of the circus, out of personal and back to the controlled world of Mathew Bond, banker.

Henry was lying in his hospital bed, and he looked old and white and defeated. Bella just looked sick.

The doctor she'd met on the way in had given her good news. 'There doesn't seem to be any damage to his heart. We're fairly sure it was simply a bad attack of angina, but your grandmother says he's losing weight. He's running a slight fever and we need to get his angina under control, so we'd like to keep him in for a few days, run a few tests, see if we can get him looking a bit stronger before we send him back to the wilds of circus living.'

He won't be going back to the wilds of circus living, Allie thought drearily, but she pushed the ward door open with her smile pinned in place and spent the first few minutes telling her grand-parents of the unlikely success of their banker as a ringmaster.

It made them smile—but the big issue couldn't be avoided.

She didn't have to bring it up. Mathew was right. Both Henry and Bella had a clear idea of what was happening, and why.

'Why didn't you tell me?' she whispered, holding her grandpa's hand, and he snorted.

'Telling you wouldn't have made a difference. We figured we'd keep the circus cheerful and functioning right up till the moment they pulled the rug.'

Great, Allie thought bleakly. They had two weeks of advance bookings. Almost every show for the time they were in Fort Neptune was sold out. She couldn't conceive of folding the big top tomorrow and leaving a gap in the heart of the town at the height of summer.

She couldn't bear thinking today had been their last day.

And wages? To go back to the crew now and say it's over, no more pay as of now...

Was there any money to pay wages already owed? She should have asked. She should have demanded to see what powers Mathew had.

Her head was spinning, and Bella put her wrinkled hand on hers so there were three hands combined, Henry's, Bella's and Allie's. 'It's okay, dear,' she said. 'Something will come up.'

'Something already has come up,' she muttered. 'Mathew Bond.'

'But he has to be a nice young man. He's the great-nephew of Margot and Margot's lovely. Why don't you talk to her?'

'Mathew says she's dying.'

There was a pause at that. A really long pause. Then...

'Just because you're dying, it doesn't mean you're dead,' Bella said at last, with a lot more asperity than usual. 'Your grandpa and I are almost eighty and if people treat us like we're on our last legs we might as well be. Don't you think Margot would want to know how appallingly her nephew is acting?'

'He has the right...'

'The moral right?' Bella said. 'Maybe he has and maybe he hasn't. We've given his aunt a lot of pleasure over the years. At least he can let us have our last two weeks here without refunding tickets. Bond's is huge. Our loan must be a drop in the ocean. Go and see Margot, love. Talk to her.'

'But she's dying,' Allie repeated, horrified.

'Yes, but she's not dead,' Bella repeated impatiently. 'Just like our circus isn't dead until we take down the big top. And just like your grandpa isn't dead yet. He'll be fine, Allie, love, as long as he has hope.'

'That's blackmail. You want me to front a dying Margot and her cashmere-coated nephew so Grandpa will get better?'

'That's the one,' Bella said and beamed.

'You're such a good girl,' Henry said and gave a wee feeble cough and sank further back into his pillows.

Allie glared. 'You're a fraud. Grandpa, was that collapse real this afternoon?'

'Of course it was,' Henry said, affronted, possibly with stronger affront than the wee feeble cough signified should be possible.

'Go and see Margot, Allie,' Bella urged. 'It's the least you can do.'

'I...'

'At least talk again to the nephew.'

She did have to do that. There were so many complications.

'Do you know where Margot lives?' Henry asked. 'The second house from the point along the esplanade. It's a little blue fisherman's cottage.'

'You've been there before—asking for money?'

'I had to keep the animals safe,' Henry said,

and suddenly his old eyes were steel. 'I did that for you.'

And he had, Allie thought. Henry was an old-fashioned ringmaster, with old-fashioned views on circus animals. It was her distress that had made him retire them.

It was her distress that had put them into this mess?

'They're still okay,' she said carefully, feeling weird.

'We know. We get updates,' Bella said, beaming. She dived into her purse and produced photographs, and Allie found herself staring at pictures of lions and monkeys and two gorgeous, healthy elephants. Maisie and Minnie. She'd adored these animals as a kid. She'd fought for them.

That fight had got them into this mess. What would happen to them now?

'You need to talk to Margot,' Bella urged again, and Allie shook her head.

'I need to talk to Mathew.'

'Same thing,' Bella retorted. 'He's staying with her.'

'How do you know?'

'Of course we know. We were expecting...'

'Enough.' Allie put up her hands in surrender. 'I

don't want to know what you were expecting. At least, I do want to know, but I'm not the least sure I can trust you two. I may not want to trust Mathew Bond either, but at least he gives me facts. I'll see him. Meanwhile, you stay well, both of you, and no more conniving. I'll do my best to see what I can save, but you need to leave it in my hands.'

She kissed them both and left. She headed down to the beach and took herself for a really long walk. She thought about elephants and lions and monkeys. She thought about a circus she loved, a team she loved. She thought about a circus sold out for two solid weeks.

And then she went to face Mathew.

CHAPTER THREE

MARGOT'S HOUSE WAS adorable. This whole town was adorable, Allie thought, as she walked past the long row of fishermen's cottages to reach Margot's postcard-perfect cottage.

The rain had stopped. The late afternoon sun was shimmering on the water and the boats swinging at anchor in the bay looked clean and washed. Fort Neptune had once been a major defence port, and the fort itself was still a monolith on the far headland, but the time for defence was long past. The town was now a sleepy fishing village that came alive each summer, filling with kids, mums and dads eager for time out from the rest of the world.

It was Allie's very favourite circus site, and the thought that Henry and Bella had planned their retirement here was a comfort.

Or it had been a comfort, she thought grimly, fighting for courage to bang Margot's lion-shaped brass knocker. It was all lies.

Lies created to save her elephants?

This was her call. Her responsibility. She took a deep breath—and knocked.

Mathew answered, looking incongruously big, stooping a little in the low doorway. Margot's forebears must have been little, Allie thought—or maybe it was just Mathew was large. Or not so much large as powerful. He was wearing a fisherman's guernsey and jeans. Maybe he'd walked on the beach as well—he looked windswept and tousled and…and…

Okay, he looked gorgeous, she conceded, taking a step back, but gorgeous didn't have any place here. He was looking at her as if she was a stranger, as if she had no right to be here, and she felt like running.

If Margot was dying she had no right to intrude.

But what was at stake was her grandparents' future and the future of all the crew. If she didn't front this man she'd have to go back to the showground, give orders to dismantle the big top and do…what?

The future stretched before her like a great, empty void.

'I need to talk to you,' she said, but Mathew's face was impassive. She was a loan, she thought.

A number on a balance sheet. A red one. It was this guy's job to turn it to black.

The human side of him had emerged this afternoon. Her grandfather's collapse had propelled him into the circus ring and he'd done well, but how could she propel him to do more?

The loan was enormous. She had the collateral of an ageing circus and a bunch of weird animals. Nothing else.

He needed to turn back into a banker and she knew it.

'There's nothing more I can do,' he said, surprisingly gently. 'But how's your grandpa?'

'I…he's okay. They're keeping him in hospital for checks.'

'Maybe it's just as well. It'll keep him off site while the circus is disbanded.'

She felt sick. More, she felt like…like…

No. She had no idea what she felt like. Her world was spinning, and she had no hope of clinging to it.

'Mathew?' She recognised the old lady's voice calling from the living room. Margot. 'Mathew, who is it?'

'It's Allie from the circus,' she called back before Mathew could answer. Margot had always seemed a friend. It would have been wrong not to answer. 'It's Allie, alias The Amazing Mischka.'

There was a faint chuckle in return. 'Mischka. Allie. Come on in, girl.'

Come in...

'How sick is she?' she said urgently, whispering.

'She's decided she's dying,' Mathew said in an under-voice. 'She's only eighty, but her dog died and she's scarcely eaten since. She's spending her time planning her funeral and deciding who inherits her pot plants. Not me, I gather, because I'm not responsible enough. It sounds comic but it's not. She wants to die, and she's making sure it happens.'

'Oh, no.' She looked into his impassive face— and realised it wasn't impassive. He was fond of the old lady, then. Very fond.

'Come in, girl.' Margot's voice was imperative. 'Mathew, don't keep her out there.'

'Don't...' Mathew said and then he shrugged his shoulders. But she knew what he wanted to say. *Don't upset her. This loan is nothing to do with her.*

'Allie!' This time the call was peremptory and Allie had no choice but to brush by Mathew and walk through into the sitting room. She was tinglingly, stupidly aware of Mathew as she brushed past him—but then she saw Margot and Mathew was forgotten.

Margot was sitting hunched over the fire, in a pale pink dressing gown, draped in a cashmere throw.

Allie had met this lady every year, every time the circus came to town. She was tall and dignified, wearing tailored tweeds with effortless grace. For the last few years she'd carried and used a magnificent ebony walking cane and she'd given the impression of timeless beauty.

But now she was shrivelled. Disappearing?

'Oh, Margot.' Her cry of distress was out before she could stop herself. She'd always referred to Margot as Miss Bond. They'd greeted each other with businesslike pleasantries—this woman was a patron of the circus and her grandfather's friend—but here, in her pink robe, her body hunched over the fire, Miss Bond seemed inappropriate and cruel.

She hadn't realised, she thought, how much this lady was part of her history. Even as a little girl, every time the circus was in Fort Neptune she remembered Margot in her tweeds, sitting proudly upright in the front row.

Could she remember Mathew coming with her? No. He'd be older than she was, she thought, and he mustn't have come with his aunt for years.

All these things flickered through her mind as she knelt by Margot and took her hand. 'Oh, Margot...' she said. 'Oh, Grandpa will be so distressed.'

'Your grandfather's ill himself,' Margot said, looking down at their linked hands for a moment and then gently pulling away. 'All my friends are dying.'

It was a shocking statement, one that made Allie sit back and glance at Mathew.

His face was grim.

'You still have family,' he said. 'And friends. What about Duncan? What about me? Just because you lost your dog...Margot, there's no need for you to die as well.'

'Halibut *was* my family,' she said, gently reproving. 'And it's my time. Losing Halibut made me realise it. I'm eighty years old, which is too old to get another dog. I have no intention of lying around until everyone's forgotten me and even my nephew's wrinkled and gnarled as he stands by my grave.'

It was such a ridiculous image that Allie stared

at Mathew in astonishment. He looked anything but gnarled.

He was thirty-fivish, she thought, surely not more.

'Wow,' she said to Margot. 'You might have a few more years before that happens. Too old to get another dog? Dogs live for less than fifteen years. Ninety-five isn't such a great age. And Mathew, gnarled? It doesn't seem an immediate danger.' And she chuckled.

Okay, maybe a chuckle was inappropriate. Mathew surely looked as if it was inappropriate. 'Your business is with me,' he snapped. 'Not with Margot. Come into the study.'

'Not yet,' Margot said, with a touch of the asperity Allie remembered. 'How's Henry? Mathew told me he was taken ill.'

'He'll be okay,' Allie told her, deciding to ignore Mathew's blatant disapproval. 'The doctors say it's just angina after a dose of the flu.' She looked cautiously at Margot, wondering exactly what the matter was. 'If you'd like to risk a few more years to stay friends with him, it might be worthwhile.'

Margot chuckled then, too, but it was a bitter chuckle. 'But Henry's only here in summer,' she

said. 'You all go. Two weeks of Sparkles Circus…
I can't stick around until next year.'

'And we won't be here next year, anyway,' Allie
admitted, and saw Mathew's face darken and
thought…uh oh. Hasn't he told Margot what he's
doing?

'In the study,' he snapped and it was a command,
but Margot's hand closed on Allie's wrist.

'Why not?'

'Because the circus is bankrupt,' Mathew said
in a goaded voice. 'Because they've been living on
borrowed time and borrowed money for ten years
now. Because their time has past.'

'Like mine,' Margot said, and her voice matched
his. Goaded and angry.

'You know that's not true.' Mathew closed his
eyes, as if searching for something. He sighed and
then opened them, meeting Margot's gaze head-
on. 'How can you say your time is past? You know
you're loved. You know I love you.'

It hurt, Allie thought. She watched his face as he
said it and she thought it really hurt to say those
words. *You know I love you.* It was as if he hated
admitting it, even to himself.

'And I love Sparkles Circus!' Margot retorted,

her old eyes suddenly speculative. 'You're declaring them bankrupt?'

'He has the right,' Allie admitted, deciding a girl had to be fair. 'Margot, you've been wonderful. I gather you persuaded Bond's to finance us all those years ago. I'm so grateful.'

'Yet you come here looking for more,' Mathew demanded and there was such anger in his voice that she stared at him in astonishment—and so did Margot. Whoa.

'I'm not here looking for more money,' Allie said through gritted teeth. 'Or…not much. I didn't know about the loan, but I've been through Grandpa's files now and I'm horrified. The circus can't keep going—I know that now—but what I want is permission to continue for the two weeks we're booked to perform in Fort Neptune. We have sold-out audiences. That'll more than pay our way. If we need to refund everyone, it'll eat into your eventual payout and we'll have a town full of disappointed kids. If we can keep going for two weeks then I can give the crew two weeks' notice. The alternative is going back tonight and saying clear out, the circus is over and letting your vultures do their worst.'

'Vultures…'

'Okay, not vultures,' she conceded. 'Debt collectors. Asset sellers. Whatever you want to call them. Regardless, it's a shock and we need time to come to terms with it.'

'You're foreclosing on the loan?' Margot said faintly. 'On my loan?'

'It's not your loan,' Mathew told his aunt. 'You asked Grandpa to make the loan to Henry and he did. The circus can't keep bleeding money. With Henry in hospital, they don't even have a ringmaster. How the...'

'We do have a ringmaster,' Allie said steadily and turned to Margot. She knew what she wanted. Why not lay it on the table? 'This afternoon your nephew put on Henry's suit and top hat and was brilliant as ringmaster. He's here to take care of you. Could you spare him for two performances a day? Just for two weeks and then it's over?'

'Mathew was your ringmaster?'

There was a loaded silence in the hot little room. Margot had been huddled in an armchair by the fire, looking almost as if she was disappearing into its depths. Suddenly she was sitting bolt upright, staring at Mathew as if she'd never seen him before. '*My Mathew was your ringmaster?*' she repeated, sounding dazed.

'He made an awesome one,' Allie said. 'You should come and see.'

'I did it once,' Mathew snapped. 'In an emergency.'

'And I couldn't come,' Margot moaned. 'I'm dying.'

'You don't look dead to me,' Allie said, and she wasn't sure why she said it, and it was probably wildly inappropriate, cruel even, but she'd said it and it was out there, like it or not. 'If you're not dead then you're alive. You could come.'

To say the silence was explosive would be an understatement. She glanced at Mathew and saw him rigid with shock.

He'd throw her out, she thought. He'd pick her up bodily and throw.

'I'm…I'm sorry,' she said at last because someone had to say something. 'I don't know how sick you are. That was…I mean, if you can't…'

'If you ate some dinner, let me help you dress, let us rug you up and use your wheelchair…' Mathew said in a voice that was really strange.

'I can't eat dinner,' Margot retorted, but it wasn't a feeble wail. It was an acerbic snap.

'You could if you wanted to.' He glared at Allie,

and back at Margot, and he looked like a man backed against a wall by two forces.

He loved this woman, Allie thought—and with sudden acuity she thought he loves her against his will. He hates it that he loves her and she's dying.

What was going on?

And he told her.

'It's Margot's decision to die,' he said, sounding goaded to the point of explosion. 'Her dog's died. Her knees don't let her walk like they used to, so she's given up. She's stopped eating and she won't see her friends. She's lost twelve kilos in the last four weeks.'

'You're kidding,' Allie said, awed. 'Twelve kilos? Wow, Margot, what sort of diet are you on? Our Exotic Yan Yan—Jenny to the rest of us—has tried every diet I've ever heard of. She's currently on some sort of grapefruit and porridge diet. Her husband keeps sneaking over to my caravan for bacon and eggs. Maybe I should send Jenny to you.'

There was another silence at that. A long one. She'd trivialised something life-threatening, Allie thought. Uh oh.

She glanced at Mathew and saw his face almost rigid with tension. How hard would it be, she thought, to watch someone you loved decide to die? And she'd made light of it. Joked.

But in for a penny, in for a pound. Why not go for it?

'It's Sunday,' she said, to no one in particular. To both of them. 'We don't play tonight, which is just as well as I'm feeling shattered, but tomorrow's another day. We're in the middle of the summer holidays and the forecast is for perfect weather. We have performances at two and at seven-thirty. Choose one. Mathew could rug you up and we'd keep the best seat for you like we always do. You could watch Mathew being wonderful and afterwards you could talk to Jenny about your diet.'

'You can't want me being wonderful,' Mathew exploded. 'If you think I'm about to make a spectacle of myself again…'

'You enjoyed it,' she said flatly. 'Tell me you didn't. I won't believe you.' She turned back to Margot. 'Mathew took to ringmaster to the manor born,' she said. 'He's seriously awesome. He could spend the next two weeks playing ringmaster. You could put off dying for a couple of weeks. I could give the team time to figure where we go from here. It's win-win for everyone.'

'You think dying's a whim?' Margot said faintly

and Allie took a deep breath and met her gaze head on. She'd been blunt and insensitive—why not just keep on going?

'I guess dying's something we all have to do,' Allie admitted. 'But if you could squeeze in a couple more weeks of living and lend us your nephew while you did, we'd be very grateful. More than grateful. You'd be saving the circus. You'd be giving us—all of us—one last summer.'

'The loan's already called in,' Mathew snapped.

'Then call it out again,' Margot snapped back and suddenly the old lady was pushing herself to her feet, unsteady, clinging to the arms of her chair but standing and looking from Mathew to Allie and back again.

'Mathew is your ringmaster?' she demanded as if she was clarifying details.

'He is,' Allie said.

'I'm not,' Mathew said, revolted.

'If I eat,' Margot said. 'If I manage to eat my dinner and eat my breakfast...if I decide not to die... would you extend the loan for the two weeks Allie's asking? You know I've never touched Bond's money. You know I fought with my family. Apart from that one loan to Sparkles, I've never asked anything of you or your father or your grandfather. I've asked nothing but this, but I'm asking it now.'

'Margot…'

'I know,' she said, and amazingly she grinned and Allie caught the glimpse of the old Margot, the Margot who'd been a friend of the circus forever, who'd sat and cheered and eaten hot dogs and popcorn and looked totally incongruous in her dignified tweeds but who now held the fate of the circus in her elderly, frail hands. 'It's blackmail,' she admitted. 'It's something we women are good at. Something this Allie of yours seems to exemplify.'

'She's not *my* Allie,' Mathew snapped.

'She's your leading lady,' Margot said serenely. 'Mathew, I'm happy to live for another two weeks, just to enjoy the circus.'

'This is business, Margot.'

'It's probably not fair,' Allie ventured. To say she was feeling gobsmacked would be an understatement. She'd come to plead for a two-week extension, not to negotiate a life. 'Margot, you don't have to do this.'

'Don't you want me to live?' Margot demanded, and Allie felt flummoxed and looked at Mathew and he was looking flummoxed, too.

'I came down to spend time with you,' he managed.

'And now you can,' Margot retorted. 'Only instead of immersing yourself in your financial dealings while I die, you can be a ringmaster while I watch. You've been a banker since the day you were born. Why not try something else?'

What had she done? Allie thought faintly. She hadn't just backed this man against the wall; she'd nailed him there. He was looking as if he had no choice at all.

Which was a good thing, surely? It was the fate of the whole circus team she was fighting for here. She had no space to feel sorry for him.

Besides, he was a big boy.

And he was an awesome ringmaster.

'I brought the scripts for the clown jokes for the week,' she ventured, sort of cautiously. The room still felt as if it could explode any minute. 'We swap them around because lots of families come more than once. If you could read them...even memorise them like you did today...'

'He memorised his lines?' Margot demanded.

'He helped with the water cannon joke,' Allie told her. 'He timed it to perfection.'

'My Mathew...a ringmaster...'

'Worth living for?' Allie asked and chuckled and glanced at Mathew and thought chuckling was about as far from this guy's mindset as it was possible to get.

'Yes,' Margot said. 'Yes, it is. Mathew, do you agree?'

It felt as if the world held its breath. Allie had almost forgotten how to breathe. Breathing was unnecessary, she thought—unless the decision came down on her side.

'Yes,' Mathew said at last, seemingly goaded past endurance, and she couldn't believe she'd heard right.

'Yes?'

'Give me the scripts.'

'You mean it?'

'I don't,' he said through gritted teeth, 'say anything I don't mean. Ever.'

'Oh, my…' Her breath came out in a huge rush. 'Oh, Mathew…'

'You have what you want,' he said. 'Now leave.'

'But I'd like crumpets,' Margot interjected, suddenly thoughtful. 'With butter and honey. Mathew, could you pop across to the store to get me some?'

'Of course.' Mathew sounded totally confused. 'But…'

'And leave Allie with me while you go,' she said. 'If I'm not dying I need company.'

'I'll get them for you,' Allie offered but Margot suddenly reached out and took her hand. Firmly.

'I'd like to talk to you. Without Mathew.'

'Margot…' Mathew said.

'Women's business,' Margot said blandly. 'Fifteen minutes, Mathew, then I'll eat my crumpets and have a nap and you can go back to your work. But I need fifteen minutes' private time with Allie.'

'There's nothing you need to discuss with Allie. Two weeks. That's it, Margot. No more.'

'That's fine,' Margot said serenely. 'But I will talk to Allie first. Go.'

He went. There didn't seem a choice. He needed to buy what Margot required, leaving the women to…women's business?

He had no idea what Margot wanted to talk to Allie about, but he suspected trouble. Margot was a schemer to rival Machiavelli. For the last few months she'd slumped. He'd seen how much weight she'd lost, he'd watched her sink into apathy and he really believed she was dying.

Did he need to fund a circus in perpetuity to keep her alive?

It wouldn't work, though, he thought, even if it made financial sense—which it didn't. For the next two weeks, Sparkles would play in Fort Neptune, Margot would see him as the ringmaster and maybe she'd improve. But even if the circus was fully funded, it'd move on and she'd slump again.

Meanwhile, two weeks with Allie…

Allie.

He gave himself a harsh mental shake, disturbed about where his thoughts were taking him. The last couple of days while he'd been here, watching Margot fade, he'd become…almost emotional.

What was it about a girl in a pink leotard with sparkling stripes that made him more so?

A man needed a beer, he thought, and glanced at his watch. Two minutes down, thirteen minutes to go. Women's business. What were they talking about?

A man might even need two beers.

'You need to excuse my nephew.' With the door safely closed behind Mathew, Margot lost no time getting to the point. 'He doesn't cope with emotion.'

'Um…' Allie was disconcerted. 'I don't think

I need to excuse Mathew for anything. He's just saved our circus.'

'For two weeks and he foreclosed in the first place.'

'Grandpa borrowed the money,' she admitted, trying to be fair. 'With seemingly no hope of repaying the capital. Bond's is a bank, not a charity. It's business.'

'And that's all Mathew does,' Margot said vehemently. 'Business. His parents and sister died in a car crash when he was six. His grandfather raised him—sort of—but he raised him on his terms, as a banker. That boy's been a banker since he was six and he knows nothing else. I brought him down here for two weeks every summer and I tried my best to make him a normal little boy, but for the rest of his life…His grandfather worked sixteen-hour days—he did from the moment his son died—and he took care of Mathew by taking him with him to the bank. He taught Mathew to read the stock market almost as soon as he could read anything. Before he was ten he could balance ledgers. His grandfather—my brother—closed up emotionally. The only way Mathew could get any affection was by pleasing him, and the only way to please him was to be clever with figures. And there was nothing I could do about it. Nothing.'

'Oh, Margot…' What business was this of hers, Allie thought, but she couldn't stop her.

'You're the same, I suspect,' Margot said. 'The circus is in your blood; you've been raised to it. I've watched you as a little girl, without a mother, but I always thought having the run of the circus would be much more fun than having the run of the bank.'

'I've never…not been loved,' Allie said.

'You think I can't see that? And I bet you're capable of loving back. But Mathew… He's brought three women to visit me over the years, three women he thought he was serious about, and every one of them was as cool and calculating as he is. Romance? He wouldn't know the first thing about it. It's like…when his family was killed he put on emotional armour and he's never taken it off.'

'Why are you telling me this?' Allie asked, feeling weird. 'It's none of my business.'

'It *is* your business,' Margot said. 'You've thrown him off balance, and what my Mathew needs is to be thrown off balance and kept off balance. Knock him off his feet, girl. If you want to save your circus…'

'Margot…' She'd been sitting on a stool near Margot. Now she rose and backed away. 'No. I'm not even thinking…I wouldn't…'

'If I thought you would, I wouldn't suggest it.'

'And that makes no sense at all,' she said and managed a chuckle. 'Margot, no. I mean…would a Bond want a kid from the circus?'

'He might *need* a kid from the circus. A woman from the circus.'

Margot was matchmaking, Allie thought, aghast. One moment she'd been dying. The next, she was trying to organise a romance for her nephew.

'I think,' she said a trifle unsteadily, 'that I've won a very good deal by coming tonight. You've helped me keep the circus going for two weeks and that's all I came for. I'd also really like it if you kept on living,' she added for good measure. 'But that's all I'm interested in. You're about to eat crumpets. If you'll excuse me, I think I'll quit while I'm ahead.'

'He needs a good woman,' Margot said as she reached the door.

'Maybe he does,' Allie managed, and tugged the door open. 'But I need a ringmaster and two weeks' finance and nothing more, so you can stop your scheming this minute.'

* * *

The pub was closed. Sunday night in Fort Neptune, Matt thought morosely. Yee-ha.

He walked the beach instead.

The moon was rising over the water, the last tinge of sunset was still colouring the sky and the beauty of the little fort was breathtaking—yet he deliberately turned his mind to figures.

Figures were a refuge. Figures were where he was safe.

It had been that way for as long as he remembered.

When he was six years old his family had died. He had a vague memory of life with them, but only vague. He remembered the aftermath, though. The great Bond mausoleum. His grandfather being… stoic. His great-aunt Margot arriving and yelling, *'Someone has to cuddle the child. I know you're breaking your heart, but you're burying yourself in your bank. You have a grandson. If you can't look after him, let me have him.'*

'The boy stays with me.'

'Then look after him. Take him to the bank with you. Teach him your world. Heaven knows, it's not the perfect answer but it's better than leaving him alone. Do it.'

Thinking back, it had been an extraordinary childhood, and it didn't take brains to understand why he was now really only comfortable ensconced in his world of high finance.

Which was why this was so...bewildering. Walking on the beach in the moonlight, knowing tomorrow he'd be a ringmaster...

Figures. Business.

He needed guarantees, he thought, fighting to keep his mind businesslike. He needed an assurance that in two weeks the handover would be smooth and complete.

He'd draw up a contract. Make it official. That was the way to go.

It was a plan, and Mathew Bond was a man who worked according to plans.

Tonight he'd watch Margot eat crumpets, he'd help her to bed, and then he'd make Allie sign something watertight. He'd make sure it was clear this was a two-week deal. And then...

Okay, for two weeks he'd be ringmaster, and that was that. He hoped that it'd make a difference to Margot but if it didn't there was only so much a man could do.

He'd do it, and then he'd get back to his world.

To banking.

To a world he understood.

CHAPTER FOUR

AFTER LEAVING MARGOT, Allie headed back to the hospital. She reassured herself Henry was okay, she told her grandparents about the two weeks, she brought an exhausted and emotional Bella back to her caravan and settled her and told her the world wasn't about to end, and finally she retreated to the sanctuary of her own little van, her own little world.

Her dogs greeted her with joy. Tinkerbelle and Fairy were her own true loves. The two Jack Russell terriers were packed with loyalty and intelligence and fun.

There'd never been a time when Allie hadn't had dogs. These two were part of her act, the circus crowd went wild with their funny, clever tricks, and she adored them as much as they adored her.

She greeted them in turn. She made herself soup and toast and then she tried to watch something on the television.

It normally worked. Cuddling dogs. Mindless television.

There was no way it was settling her now. There was too much happening in her head. The loan. Grandpa. Margot.

Mathew.

And it was Mathew himself who was unsettling her most.

She had so many complications in her life right now, she did not need another one, she told herself. What was she doing? She did not need to think of Mathew Bond…like she was thinking of Mathew Bond.

'It's Margot,' she told her dogs. 'An old, dying woman playing matchmaker. She's put all sorts of nonsensical ideas into my head, and I need to get rid of them right now.'

But the ideas wouldn't go. Mathew was there, big and beautiful, front and centre.

'Maybe it's hormones,' she said and she thought maybe it was. As a circus performer, hormones didn't have much of a chance to do their stuff.

Hormones… Romance… It wasn't for the likes of Allie. She moved from town to town, never settling and, as Henry and Bella had become older, Allie's duties had become more and more onerous.

It wasn't that she wasn't interested in a love life. It was that she simply couldn't fit it in. She'd had all of three boyfriends in her life and none had lasted more than six months. Trailing after a circus performer was no one's idea of hot romance, and within the circus... Well, no one there exactly cut it in the sexy and available stakes.

'So now I'm thinking about Mathew and it's nothing but fancy, but oh, if I could...' she whispered, and for a moment, for just a fraction of a lonely evening after a hard and frightening day, she gave herself permission to fantasise.

Mathew holding her. Mathew smiling at her with that gentle, laughing smile she'd barely glimpsed but she knew was there.

Mathew taking her into his arms. Mathew...

No! If she went there, she might not be able to pull back. She had to work with the man for the next two weeks.

'This is nonsense,' she told the dogs. 'Crazy stuff. We'll concentrate on the telly like we do every night. Half an hour to settle, then bed, and we'll leave the hormones where they belong—outside with my boots.'

It was sensible advice. It was what a girl had to

do—and then someone knocked on the door of the van.

Mathew. She sensed it was him before she opened the door.

He was standing in front of her, looking slightly ruffled.

He was wearing that fabulous coat again.

Mathew.

What was he doing, standing in the grounds of the circus at nine at night, holding a contract in one hand, knocking on the door of a woman in pink sequins with the other?

This was business, he told himself fiercely—and she wouldn't be in pink sequins.

She wasn't. She was still in her jeans. Her wind-cheater was sky-blue, soft, warm and vaguely fuzzy.

She looked scrubbed clean and fresh, a little bit tousled—and very confused to see him.

The dogs were going nuts at her feet, which was just as well. It gave him an excuse to stoop to greet them and get his face in order, telling him-self again—fiercely—that he was here on business.

She stooped to hush the dogs and their noses

were suddenly inches apart. She looked…she looked…

Like he couldn't be interested in her looking. He stood up fast and stepped back.

'Good evening,' he said, absurdly formal, and he saw a twinkle appear at the back of her eyes. She could see his discomfort? *She was laughing?*

'Good evening,' she said back, rising and becoming just as formal. 'How can I help you?'

He held up his contract and she looked at it as she might look at a death adder. The twinkle died.

'What is it?'

'It's an agreement by you that these two weeks are not in any way a concession or notice by the bank that we've waived our legal rights. Our control over the circus starts now; you're here for the next two weeks on our terms.'

'I can't sign that,' she whispered. 'Grandpa…'

'You can sign it. You agreed before the show that you wouldn't interfere with foreclosure. Your grandfather has named you on the loan documents as having power of attorney but, even so, we don't actually need you to have legal rights. We don't need to disturb Henry. As the person nominally in charge right now, all we're saying is that your presence here for the next two weeks doesn't interfere with legal processes already in place.'

She pushed her fingers through her hair, brushing it back from her face. Wearily. 'Isn't that assumed?' she asked. 'That the next two weeks doesn't stop you from turning into a vulture at the end of it?'

He didn't reply, just stood and looked at her. She looked exhausted, he thought. She looked beat.

She looked a slip of a girl, too young to bear the brunt of responsibility her grandfather had placed on her.

'Have you told everyone?' he asked and she nodded.

'I asked Grandpa whether I should tell the crew, and he said yes. He's known this was coming. He should have told us and he's feeling bad. He asked me to give everyone as much notice as possible.'

So she'd had to break the bad news herself.

'I'm sorry.'

'So am I,' she said wearily. 'Do I have to sign this now?'

It could have waited until morning, he thought. Why had it seemed so important to get this on a business footing right now? Was it to make it clear—to himself more than anyone—that he wasn't being tugged into an emotional minefield?

'We might as well,' he said. 'Seeing I'm here.'

'I'll need to read it first. Are we talking a thirty page document?'

'Two.'

'Fine.' She sighed and pushed the door wide so he could enter. The dogs stood at each side of her, looking wary.

How well trained were they?

'They're not lions,' she said, following his look. 'They don't go for the jugular. They're very good at hoops, though.'

They were. He'd seen them at work today and they were amazing. They were two acrobatic canines, who now looked like two wary house pets, here to protect their mistress.

'Basket,' she said and they checked her face, as if to make sure she really meant it, then obligingly jumped into their basket.

It was tucked into a neat slot under the table where feet didn't need to go—about the only space in the van a basket would fit. The van was a mastery of a home in miniature, he thought. Unlike Bella and Henry's, it wasn't cluttered. It looked feminine and workable, and very, very comfortable.

'Nice,' he said approvingly and she gave a sort-of smile.

'It's the way we live. It'll be hard to get used to a house that doesn't move.'

'Will you work for another circus?'

'No!' That was definite. 'Most circuses are no-madic and I can't leave Gran and Grandpa. The only circus that works around here is Carvers and I won't go near them in a pink fit.'

'So what will you do?'

'I'm a trained accountant,' she said and he blinked because of all the unlikely professions...

'I know,' she added bleakly. 'I'm a qualified ac-countant for a circus that's gone bankrupt. What a joke.'

'But how can you be a qualified accountant?'

'Online university,' she said curtly. 'Doesn't that fit the image? Circus folk. Inbred and weird.'

'I never said that.'

'You never thought that? Why the astonishment, then? Because we're bankrupt? It's not my fault. Professionally, this is a bombshell. I wasn't given the facts.'

'Which wasn't fair.'

'Maybe it was,' she said wearily. 'I wasn't given the facts to protect me. Grandpa could never have afforded to keep our animals into their old age. He took on the debt for me. I loved those elephants, and even now I'll never agree to have them put down, even though I foresee a lifetime of debt in front of me.' She closed her eyes for a brief moment, as if gathering strength for a lifetime of elephant support, then took the document and sat at her table-in-miniature and read.

He stood and watched her read.

Her head was bowed over the paper. Her gorgeous curls were tumbled so he couldn't see her face.

A lifetime of debt…A lifetime of bookkeeping for a girl in pink sequins.

'There might be charities that'll help with the animals,' he ventured at last, and she nodded without looking up.

'I'll sort it. Not your problem. According to this, Bond's owns this circus and all its assets as of today—and nothing we can do in the next two weeks changes it.'

'That's right.'

'And we're in receivership right now. You'll sell us to Carvers?'

'That's up to us,' he said gently and she bit her lip and went back to reading.

'All this document says is that I promise not to try and extend the two weeks, and I don't get rid of any assets in the interim.'

'That's the gist.' She was good, he thought. What she was accepting must be a gut-wrenching shock, but he'd drawn it up in legalese, and she had it in one quick scan.

'So no riding off into the sunset on camels?'

'Um…no.' Unbelievably, she was trying to smile, and something inside him twisted. Hurt.

She read on, then reached for a pen and signed.

'We won't do anything stupid,' she said dully and the smile had gone again. He missed it.

'Thank you.' He took the document, checked the signature—some things were inbred—and tucked it into his pocket.

He should go.

'This is not your fault,' she said suddenly. 'And you have promised to be ringmaster. There's no reason for you to feel bad.'

'I don't.' But he did and she knew it. How? She was watching his face and he had a strange feeling that she could see…much more than he wanted her to see.

'I need to check on Pharaoh,' she said abruptly, standing again, and in the confines of the tiny caravan she was way too close. She'd washed in something lemony, he thought. Citrus. Nice.

He could just reach out and touch those curls.

In his dreams. He was here on business.

'Pharaoh?'

'You met him this morning. Camel. Cough.'

'Right,' he said faintly. 'Don't you have anyone else to do the heavy work?'

'The animals are mine,' she said, suddenly protective. 'I love them. How could I ask anyone else to care for them?'

'*You love camels*?'

'How can I not? Come and make their acquaintance. You've only met them in passing, and they're special.'

He should leave—but the lady of the pink sequins was asking him to go chat to camels.

How could a banker resist an invitation like that?

The ground had dried a little since this morning, but not much. His brogues were suffering. Allie had her boots on again and was sloshing along like a farmer.

She graciously allowed him to carry the feed bucket.

The enclosure was made of cyclone fencing panels, bolted together to form a secure, temporary home. The panels started and ended at a huge truck, opened at the back with the ramp down.

'That's their retreat,' Allie told him, seeing him checking the place out under the temporary lighting. 'The van's their security. The camels hardly use theirs but if they're threatened—for instance we've had hoodlums break in and throw stones, and once we had dogs dig under the fencing—they'll back into the van. The noise they make clattering up the ramp is enough to wake us and we'll be out here in minutes, but we're not worried. We seldom have problems.'

The camels didn't look worried, Mathew thought, as he saw the great beasts greet Allie with what looked almost like affection. Even though he carried the feed bucket, it was Allie they headed for.

She greeted each of them in turn, scratching ears, slapping sides, and as one tried to nuzzle her neck she reached up and hugged him.

'Pharaoh's a softie,' she told him. 'He's the oldest. His cough's getting better. I think we might let him work tomorrow.'

'It won't be too strenuous?' He thought back, remembering the clowns slipping and sliding from the camels' backs.

'They love it,' she said simply. 'These guys are designed to trudge through the desert, going without water for days at a time. I'll take them for a decent workout in the morning, but without the circus work they're bored. If they can't work...' She faltered. 'I'm going to have to find them a desert to roam.'

'On accountancy wages?'

'That's not your problem,' she said again, and grabbed the feed bucket and sloshed it into the trough with something like violence.

'We might be able to find you an accountancy position within the bank.'

He'd said it without thinking. He'd said it because...she seemed bereft. Alone. She seemed a slip of a girl with the weight of the circus on her shoulders.

He shouldn't have said it, and he knew it the moment the words were out of his mouth.

She didn't look at him, but she straightened and looked beyond the circus grounds, to the foreshore where the moon glimmered over the distant sea.

He saw her shoulders brace, just a little, as if she was preparing herself for what lay ahead.

'Thank you,' she said in a cool, polite voice that had nothing to do with the Allie he was beginning to know. 'But I have Gran and Grandpa, and my two great-uncles—Fizz and Fluffy are really Harold and Frank and they're Gran's brothers. How can I leave them? I can't. Between us we have two dogs, three camels and three ponies. So…an apartment within commuting distance of Bond's Bank… Sydney, isn't it?'

'Yes, but…'

'There you go, then. Impossible.'

'Allie…' He was supposed to be the stand-back, dispassionate banker here. Bankers didn't get involved—had his grandfather taught him nothing? But right now…

He couldn't bear it. He felt so responsible he felt ill.

He put a hand on her shoulder, but the moment he touched her she wheeled to face him. With anger.

'For the third time, it's not your problem,' she snapped, and she was so close…so close…

'I'd like to help.'

'You already are. You're ringmaster. You've extended our time. What else?'

'I could do more.'

'Like what?' His hand was still on her shoulder and she wasn't pulling away. 'Extend the loan? Let us get deeper in debt? Even if you would, we couldn't accept. I know when to call it quits and we're calling it quits now. You've given us two weeks of getting used to the idea, of finding ourselves somewhere to live, of figuring out something. The caravans will be repossessed but they're ancient, anyway. I now know why Grandpa's been so reluctant to replace or even fix them. I'm thinking maybe an old farmhouse somewhere out of town, for a peppercorn rent, some place I can commute to a bookkeeping job for a local car yard or something. You don't need to offer any more charity.'

'It's not charity.' She was still so close. His banker barriers...his rule about non-involvement... were dissolving because she was so close.

'Giving us that loan in the first place was charity,' she said bleakly. 'No more.'

'Allie...'

'What?' she demanded, and glared up at him and it was too much. It was far too much.

She was too close. The moonlight was on her face. She looked frightened and angry and brave, all three, all at the one time, and quite simply he'd never seen a woman so lovely. She stood there in her ancient jacket and old jeans and her disgusting boots, but the memory of her slim, taut body flying through the air in her pink and silver sequins was with him still.

A bookkeeper for a car yard...

His hand was on her shoulder. He could feel her breathing.

She was glaring up at him, breathing too fast. She should break away. He expected her to, but she didn't.

Why? The night held no answer. It was as if they were locked there, motionless in time and space.

One woman and one man...

Her face was just there. Her mouth was just there.

Don't get involved.

How could he not? Something was happening here that was stronger than him. He didn't understand it, but he had no hope of fighting it.

It'd take a stronger man than he was to resist, and he didn't resist.

She didn't move. She stood and looked up at him in the moonlight, anger and despair mixed, but something else...something else...

He didn't understand that look. It was something

he had no hope of understanding and neither, he thought, did she.

Loneliness? Fear? Desperation?

He knew it was none of those things, but maybe it was an emotion born of all three.

It was an emotion he'd never met before, but he couldn't question it, for there was no time here or space for asking questions. There was only this woman, looking up at him.

'Allie, I care,' he said and it was as if someone else was talking.

'How can you care?'

He had no answer. He only knew that he did.

He only knew that it felt as if a part of him was being wrenched out of place. He was a banker, for heaven's sake. He shouldn't feel a client's pain.

But this was Allie's pain. Allie, a woman he'd known for less than a day. A woman he was holding, with comfort, but something more. He looked down at her and she looked straight back up at him and he knew that now, for this moment, he wasn't her banker.

In a fraction of a moment, things had changed, and he knew what he had to do. He knew for now, for this moment in time, what was inevitable, and she did, too.

He cupped her face in his hand, he tilted her chin—and he stooped to kiss her.

One minute she was feeling sick and sorry and bereft. The next she was being kissed by one of the most gorgeous males she'd ever met.

The most gorgeous male she'd ever met. Her banker.

Her ringmaster?

It had been an appalling day. She was emotionally gutted *and he was taking advantage.*

But, right now, she wasn't arguing and he actually wasn't taking advantage. Or if he was, she *wanted* him to take advantage. If taking advantage felt like this…

It did feel like this. It felt like…It felt like…

It felt like she should stop thinking and just feel. For this moment she could stop being lonely and fearful and bereft and block every single thought out with the feel of this man's body.

His mouth was strong, warm, possessive. Persuasive. Seductive? Yes! She was being seduced and that was exactly what she wanted. She wanted to let go. She wanted to forget, and melt into this man's body with a primeval need.

For there was no fear or loneliness or bereavement in this kiss. Instead she could feel a slow burn, starting at her mouth and spreading. There was another burn starting in her toes and spreading upward, and another in her brain, spreading downward.

In her heart and spreading outward?

She'd gone too long between kisses. In a travelling circus, the opportunities for romance were few and far between. How else to explain this reaction?

But did she need to explain? Stop thinking, she told herself frantically. This is here, this is now and there's no harm. For now simply open your lips and savour.

And she had no choice, for her mouth seemed to be opening all by itself, welding to his, feeling the heat and returning fire with fire.

Her arms were wrapping round his gorgeous coat, tugging him closer, closer still. Sense had deserted her. For now all she needed was him. All she wanted was him.

Mathew.

His big hands held her, tight, hard and wonderful. Her breasts were moulding to his chest.

She could feel the faint rasp of stubble. She could smell the sheer masculine scent of him.

She could feel the beating of his heart.

She wanted… She wanted…

She didn't know what she wanted, but what she got was a camel, shoving its nose right between them and braying like an offended…camel?

This was a kiss that needed power to break, but there was something about a camel that made even the most wondrous kiss break off mid-stride.

They broke apart. Allie staggered and Mathew gripped her shoulders and held—but Pharaoh was still between them, his great head looped over their arms, moving in, an impermeable barrier between them.

She heard herself laugh—sort of—or maybe it was more of a sob. At the end of a nightmare day, this had been quite a moment. It was a moment that had lifted her out of dreary and desolate into somewhere she hadn't known existed. It had warmed her from the inside out. It had made her think…

Or not think. Just feel. That was what she'd wanted, she thought almost hysterically. It had been a miracle all by itself. For a moment she hadn't thought at all.

But what now? Pharaoh had broken Mathew's hold on her shoulders. She looked past the big camel and saw Mathew's face and she thought, he's as confused as I am.

Not possible. She was so confused she was practically a knot inside.

Or maybe she wasn't confused. Maybe what she wanted—desperately—was to shove this great lump of a camel aside and will this guy to pick her up and carry her to her caravan. Or not her caravan—that was far too pedestrian for what she was feeling now. What about a five-star hotel, with champagne and strawberries on the side?

Um…not? Sense was sweeping back and she could have wept. She didn't want sense. She wanted the fantasy. James Bond and the trimmings…

Not James Bond. Mathew Bond, banker.

'Maybe…maybe that was a bit unwise,' the banker said, in a voice that was none too steady. 'I don't make love to clients.'

And with that, any thought of luxury hotels and vast beds and champagne went right out of the window. *Client.*

'And I don't make love to staff,' she managed.

'Staff?'

'With Grandpa in hospital, I'm in charge of the circus and you're ringmaster. Staff,' she snapped and saw a glint of laughter deep in those dark eyes.

Pharaoh nudged forward as if he anticipated the need to intervene again, and Allie leaned against the camel and shoved, so both of them backed a little away from Mathew. To a safer distance.

'But the ringmaster has the whip,' Mathew said softly and, to her amazement, he was grinning.

She gasped, half astonished, half propelled to laughter. But she was grateful, she conceded. He was making light of it. She needed to keep it light.

'There's a new prop edict as of tomorrow,' she managed. 'Whips are off the agenda.'

'I guess they need to be,' he said a trifle ruefully. 'Allie, I'm sorry. I don't know what came over me.'

It needed only that. An apology.

'I don't normally…react,' she said, trying to keep her voice in order.

'To kissing?'

'To anything. You caught me at a weak moment.'

'As I said, I'm sorry.'

They were back to being formal. Absurdly formal.

'You have your contract,' she told him. 'You need to get back to Margot.'

'I do.'

'Goodnight, then,' she said and she clung to her camel. A girl had to hold on to something.

'You don't need more help?'

'I don't need anything.'

'I suspect you do,' he said, his voice gentle. 'You're so alone. But I also suspect you don't need me making love to you. You have enough complications on your plate already.'

'It was a nice kiss,' she managed. 'I quite liked it. But if you think it causes complications you're way out, Banker. One kiss does not complications make. Goodnight.'

He looked at her for a long moment and she looked right back. Firmly. Using every ounce of self-control she possessed to keep that look firm.

She was aware that Pharaoh had swivelled as well, so both of them were staring.

One girl and one camel...the man didn't have a chance.

'Goodnight, then, Allie,' he said gently. 'And to you, too, Pharaoh. Sleep well, and let any complications rest until tomorrow.'

'You're not a complication,' Allie snapped.

'I meant bankruptcy,' he said, even more gently. 'I mean the disbanding of your circus as well as your way of life. I didn't mean me at all.'

And he reached out and touched her, a feather touch, a faint tracing of one strong finger down the length of her cheekbone.

'I need to come early tomorrow to look through

your books,' he said softly, as if hauling himself back to reality. Hauling himself away from…complications? 'I'm sorry, but you're right, this is business. We'll make it as easy as possible, though. No whips at all.'

CHAPTER FIVE

HE'D COME TO Fort Neptune to say goodbye to his great-aunt. Instead, he was watching her pack away a comprehensive breakfast and listening to her nudge him in the direction of romance.

'She's lovely. I've thought she was lovely ever since she was a wee girl. Her grandpa used to pop her on the back of the ponies in her pink tulle and she was so cute...'

'I'm not in the market for a woman in pink tulle,' he growled and she grimaced.

'You'd prefer black corporate? Honestly, Mathew, that last woman you brought down here...'

'Angela was caught up in a meeting and didn't have time to change before leaving. She changed as soon as she got here.'

'Into black and white corporate lounge wear. And she refused to go for a walk on the beach. Mathew, just because you lost your parents and sister, it doesn't mean you can't fall in love. Properly, I mean.'

'There's the pot calling the kettle black,' he growled. 'Your Raymond never came back from the war and you dated again how many times? And that guy who calls every morning and you refuse to see him…Duncan. He's a widower, he's your age, he has dogs who look exactly the same as Halibut…'

'They are not the same. They're stupid.'

'They look the same.'

'They come from the same breeder,' she said stiffly. 'Those dogs of Allie's came from him, too. Allie got the smart ones. I got Halibut and he was the best. Duncan got what was left over.'

'You're changing the subject.'

'*You're* changing the subject,' she retorted. 'We were talking about your love life.'

He sighed. 'Okay. We're two of a kind,' he said grimly. 'We both know where love left us, so maybe we should leave it at that. But are you coming to watch today?' But he thought…they'd never had a conversation like this. About love?

When he'd mentioned Duncan, Margot had looked troubled. Why? Had he touched a nerve?

A love life? Margot?

'Tomorrow,' she said. 'My knees are still wobbly.'

'Because you've hardly eaten for months.'

'My decision not to keep on living is sensible,' she said with dignity, and he grimaced.

'It's dumb. There are always surprises round the corner.'

'Like you'd notice them. Corporate...'

'I am,' he said in a goaded voice, 'spending most of my day today with pink sparkles.'

'So you are,' she said, cheering up, and in silent agreement both of them put the moment of un-characteristic questioning aside. 'For two weeks. I hope I'll be fit to come tomorrow and if I can I'll come every day until the end.'

The end...

The words hung and emotion slammed back into the room again.

The end of the circus?

'You won't go back to dying at the end of the circus, will you?' he demanded.

'You won't go back to corporate?'

'That's not fair.'

'It is fair,' she retorted. 'What's the alternative? Look at you, a banker all your life and nothing else, and will you look at an alternative? Why not get serious about some pink sparkles? It could just change your life.'

'Like you're changing your life?'

'That's not fair, and you know it.' Then she hesitated. 'No,' she said slowly. 'Just because I make mistakes, it doesn't mean you need to join me.'

'Margot...'

'Shoo,' she said. 'Go. I've made my mistakes. You go right ahead and make yours.'

He needed to go to the circus, get into those books and make sure the structure was ready for handover, but the conversation with Margot had unsettled him. Instead, he decided on a morning walk and the walk turned into a run. He had energy to burn.

He had emotion to burn.

Margot was matchmaking. It needed only that. He'd spent half the night awake, trying to figure out how he was feeling, he was no closer now, and Margot's words had driven his questions deeper.

Allie.

Why had he kissed her? There'd been no reason at all for him to take her face between his hands, tilt her lips to his and kiss her—and Mathew Bond didn't do things without a reason.

Nor did he get involved.

Thirty years ago, aged six, Mathew had been a kid in a nice, standard nuclear family. He had a mum and a dad and a big sister, Elizabeth—Lizzy—who bossed him and played with him and made all right with his world. Sure, his father was a busy banker and his mum was corporate as well, but he and Lizzy felt secure and beloved.

That all changed one horrendous night when a truck driver went to sleep at the wheel. Mathew was somehow thrown out into the darkness. The others...Who knew? No one talked of it.

He'd woken in hospital, with his Great-Aunt Margot holding him.

'Mum? Dad? Lizzy?'

He remembered Margot's tweed coat against his cheek and somehow even at six, he hadn't needed her to tell him.

After that, his grandfather had simply taken him over. Mathew was, after all, the heir to Bond's. From the warmth, laughter, the rough and tumble of family life, he'd been propelled into his grandfather's austere existence, and he'd been stranded there for life.

He learned pretty fast to be self-contained. He had two weeks every summer with Margot, but even then he learned to stay detached. He needed to, because when the holidays ended he woke up once again in his great, barren bedroom in his grandfather's mausoleum of a house. He'd learned some pain was unbearable, and he'd learned the way to avoid it was to hold himself in.

His aunt Margot cried at the end of each summer holiday but he didn't. He didn't do emotion.

And now... He'd come down here trying to figure how to keep himself contained while Margot died. Instead, Margot was dithering over whether to die or not, his self-containment was teetering and a girl/woman in pink sequins was messing with his self-containment even more.

So why had he kissed her?

Lunacy.

Margot was right, he conceded, in her criticism of the women he dated. Inevitably they were corporate colleagues who used him as an accessory, the same way he used them. Sometimes it was handy to have a woman on his arm, and sometimes he enjoyed a woman's company, but not to the point of emotional entanglement.

And not with a woman who wore her heart on her pink spangled sleeve.

It was Margot causing this confusion, he decided. His distress for his great-aunt had clouded his otherwise cool judgement. Well, that distress could be put aside. For the time being Margot had decided to live.

Because of Allie?

Because she had renewed interest, he told himself. So… He simply had to find her more interests that weren't related to the circus.

The circus meant Allie.

No. The circus was a group of assets on a balance sheet and those assets were about to be dispersed. Allie was right. Carvers, a huge national circus group with Ron Carver at its head, was circling. The bank had put out feelers already and Carvers could well buy the circus outright.

Keeping Allie on?

This was not his business. Allie was nothing to do with him, he told himself savagely. The way she'd felt in his arms, the way she'd melted into him, had been an aberration, a moment of weakness on both their parts.

He didn't want any woman complicating his life.

He didn't want…Allie?

He jogged on. Soon he needed to head back to Margot's, get himself together and go to the circus.

Actually he was already at the circus. He'd been jogging and thinking and suddenly the circus was just over the grassy verge separating fairground from sea.

And he could see Allie.

Allie was standing by the circus gates, talking vehemently to a policeman.

The policeman had a gun.

Yeah, okay, policemen with guns didn't normally spell trouble, though they usually kept them well holstered. Maybe this was a cop organising tickets for his kids to see a show. Or not.

The gun, the body language and the look on Allie's face had Matt's strides lengthening without him being conscious of it, and by the time he reached them he figured this was trouble.

The cop looked young, almost too young to be operating alone, but then, Fort Neptune wasn't known for trouble. The towns further along the coast would be teeming with holidaymakers. The bigger towns had nightclubs. The police force would be stretched to the limit, so maybe it made sense to leave one junior cop on duty in this backwater.

What was wrong? He was surveying the circus as he jogged towards them.

The big top looked okay but something was different. He took a second to figure what it was, then realised a section of the cyclone fencing forming the camels' enclosure was flattened. The truck's doors were wide open but the truck was empty.

No camels.

He reached them and Allie gripped his arm as if she feared drowning.

'The camels…' she gasped. 'Matt, you need to stop him.' She sounded as if she'd been running. Instinctively his arm went round her and held, drawing her into him.

'Stop what? What's happened to the camels?' he asked, holding her tight.

'They're at large,' the cop snapped. 'Wild animals. You're holding me up, miss. I need to be out looking.'

'The crew's out looking,' she said, distressed. 'And they're not wild.'

'The report I received said three wild animals.'

'Tell me what's happening,' Matt said in the tone he used when meetings were threatening to get out of control. 'Now.'

There was a moment's silence. The cop looked as if he was barely contained. He was little more than a kid, Matt thought, and a dangerous one at that. Any minute now he'd be off, sirens blazing, on a camel hunt. Wanted, dead or alive...

'Someone broke into the enclosure,' Allie managed. 'They used bolt cutters to drop the cyclone fencing. But I don't understand why they've run, why they didn't just back into the truck. They're tame,' she said again to the cop. 'They're pussy cats. Who told you they're wild?'

'No matter,' the cop said brusquely. 'I'll find them.' He moved towards his car, but suddenly Matt was squarely between cop and car.

'I'm not sure what's going on,' Matt said mildly, but he motioned to the gun. 'But if you plan to shoot anything—*anything*—without a life or death reason—then I'll have your superiors down on you like a ton of bricks.' He'd started soft but his words grew firmer and slower with each syllable. This was Mathew Bond, Chairman of Bond's Bank, oozing authority at each word. 'That's a promise. Allie, is everyone out looking?'

'Yes. I just came back...Constable Taylor said...'

Enough. He didn't want to know what this spotty kid had said. He didn't need to—he could tell by Allie's body language. 'Does everyone have a phone?' he demanded. 'Does the crew have them?

Will they phone you, Allie, as soon as the camels are located?'

'Y...yes.'

'And if a member of the public phones, they'll contact you, Constable Taylor?'

'A message will be relayed to me,' the cop said ponderously.

'Excellent,' Matt said and hauled open the passenger door to the front of the patrol car. 'Allie, you ride up front and watch. Constable, you drive, and I'll ride lookout in the back.'

'Lookout?' Allie said faintly and he managed a reassuring grin.

'I'll be riding sidekick to a cop,' he said. 'I've been waiting for a chance to do this all my life. Let's go.'

Riding sidekick? Had he just said that? What did he think this was, the Wild West? But there was no way he was letting this gun-happy cop off on a camel quest with no supervision.

'What gives you the right?' the cop demanded, looking stunned.

'Because I'm the circus master,' he snapped. 'Miss Miski will confirm it. These are my animals and my responsibility, and if you hurt them you'll answer to me.'

* * *

The camels had scattered. The cop drove up and down the side streets, with Allie growing more and more anxious, until they received their first call.

Caesar was out on the highway. He'd obviously reacted in panic when he'd first seen the traffic and he was almost two miles out of town. Fizz— Frank—and Fluffy—Harold—had found him. Harold was staying with him, he reported to Allie, while Frank headed back for the trailer to fetch him.

One camel safe.

'One down,' Matt said gently. 'Two more coming up.'

He was sitting in the back seat while they searched, scanning like Allie and the cop were doing, but Allie thought he was doing more than than scanning. He'd calmed things down.

The cop was still looking grim but he was also looking contained, no longer like a boy on a vigilante hunt.

Another call. Jenny and Greg had found Pharoah in a community garden. Pharoah seemed frightened, he had a minor wound on his back, but there was enough enticement in the garden to make a camel think twice about escape. Jenny and Greg took up sentry duty. The trailer would pick him up second, Allie decreed, and turned and found Matthew smiling at her.

'Two safe,' he said. 'One more and we're home free.'

She relaxed a little more, but she was still on edge. The cop's gun was in his holster right by her side. She had an almost irresistible urge to grab it and toss it out of the window.

Mathew's hand touched her shoulder, a feather touch of reassurance.

'Camels are pretty hard to hide,' he said. 'And we're right beside the only gun in town.'

She closed her eyes for a millisecond, infinitely grateful that he was here, that he was right. Australia's rigid gun laws meant no one was going to shoot, and all they had to do was find Cleo.

And finally, blessedly, her phone rang again. It was Bernie—Bernardo the Breathtaking. Allie had the phone on speaker and she sensed his distress the moment she answered.

Cleo was in the yard of the local primary school. Bleeding from a graze on her flank. Edgy. Surrounded by excited kids.

'Isn't the school closed for holidays?' Mathew

demanded of the cop as the car did a U-turn and the cop switched on the siren.

'It's used for a school holiday programme,' the cop snapped. 'For kids whose parents work. There'll be twenty kids there, from twelve years old down. A couple of student teachers run it. They're kids themselves. They'll have no hope of keeping the children safe.'

And the threat was back.

Fort Neptune was a sleepy holiday resort where the town's only cop must spend most of his time fighting boredom. Now Mathew could practically see the adrenalin surge. He had his foot down hard, his lights were flashing, his siren blazing, and Mathew thought this was a great way to approach a scared animal. *Not.*

'There's no panic,' Mathew told him. 'It's just a camel.'

'It's wild and wounded,' the cop said with conviction—and relish? 'I need to keep the kids safe at all cost.'

Then they were at the school, pulling up in a screech of tyres. The cop was out of the car with his gun drawn, but Matt was right there beside him.

It wasn't pretty.

Mathew had watched Cleo yesterday. She'd been a teddy bear of a camel, with ponies and dogs jumping over and under her, but now she did indeed look wild. The school yard was rimmed with high wire fencing. There was one open gate. How unlucky was it that she'd found it? There was no way a frightened Cleo could find it now to get back out.

And she was surrounded. Kids were shouting and pressing close and then running away, daring each other to go closer, closer. A couple of teenage girls were flapping ineffectually amongst them.

Bernie was trying to approach Cleo, trying to shoo the kids back, putting himself between the camel and the kids, but Cleo seemed terrified beyond description.

Any minute now she could rush at the kids to try and find a way to escape. Any minute now they could indeed have a tragedy.

The cop was raising his arm—with gun attached.

'You shoot in a schoolyard, you risk a ricochet that'll kill a kid. Put it down!' Mathew snapped, with all the authority he could muster, and the cop let the gun drop a little and looked doubtful instead of intent.

So far, so good.

But action was required. 'Officer, do something,' one of the older girls yelled. 'If any of these kids get hurt...'

They well could if they kept panicking Cleo, Mathew thought.

Allie was flying across the schoolyard, calling Cleo to her, but Cleo was past responding. She was backing, rearing against the fence, lurching sideways and back again. Everything was a threat.

If the kids would only stop yelling...

Maybe it was time for a man—without a gun—to take a stand.

Once upon a time, as a kid with no home life to speak of, Mathew had joined his school's army cadet programme. He hadn't stayed long—drills and marching weren't for him—but there'd been an ex-sergeant major who'd drilled them. The sergeant major could make raw recruits jump and quiver, and Mathew took a deep breath and conjured him now.

'Attention!'

He yelled with all the force he could muster. Every single kid there seemed to jump and quiver. Even Cleo jumped and quivered. He'd had no choice, but it killed him that he'd frightened her more. She backed hard against the fence and her eyes rolled back in her head.

There was blood on her flank. What sort of wound?

But there was no time for focusing on Cleo. He needed to get these kids in order before anyone could get near her.

'Everyone behind me,' he ordered, still in his sergeant major voice. 'And you...' He pointed to a pudgy boy with a stone in his hand and his arm raised. 'You throw that and I'll hurl you straight into the police car and lock the door. That's a promise. Put it down and get behind me. Every single one of you. Now!'

And, amazingly, they did. Twenty or so kids—plus the two teenage helpers—backed silently, shocked to silence.

Which left Cleo still hard against the fence, with Allie and Bernie to deal with her. But Bernie was obviously not an animal trainer. He was looking at the camel's rolling eyes and he was backing, too.

Maybe he was right, Matt conceded. The camel was huge, lanky, way higher than Allie. Allie looked almost insignificant.

But Allie could deal, Matt thought. She must. Matt's job was to keep his troops under control.

He should order them to return to their class-room, he thought, and they'd probably go—but there was one complicating factor. He could see from a glance at the teenage attendants what he was dealing with. They looked almost hysterical. Left like this, he knew the story that'd fly around town. He could see the headlines tomorrow—wild animal loose in schoolyard, threatening the safety of our children.

He needed to defuse it, now.

Besides, the cop was still waving his gun. Get rid of the kids and the way would be safe for a single bullet...

He glanced back at Allie. She knew what the stakes were. She knew what was likely to happen, but all her attention was on Cleo. She was whispering to the camel, standing still, blocking everything else out, simply talking to a creature she must know so well...

Okay, Allie on camel duty, Mathew on the rest. Defusing hysterics and rendering one gun harmless.

It was time to turn from sergeant major to schoolteacher.

'Girls and boys, we need your assistance,'

Mathew said. 'Can you help? Put up your hand if you will.'

A few hands went up. More kids looked nervously towards Cleo.

'This camel is called Cleopatra,' Mathew continued, ignoring everyone but the kids. 'She's a lovely, gentle girl camel who works in the circus you've all seen down by the beach. Today she's been injured so she's terrified. Look at her side. She's bleeding. We need to get her to the vet. Mischka is trying to calm her down. Have any of you been to the circus yet? Mischka wears pink sequins and rides on Cleo's back. She looks a bit different now, doesn't she? Do you recognise her?'

A few more hands were raised. Wounds, vet, circus—he had their attention.

'Mischka looks worried,' Mathew said, almost conversationally. 'That's because she's been out searching for Cleo for hours. Did you know Cleopatra has a special place in Mischka's heart? Cleo's mother was killed by a road train—do you know that a road train is? It's a huge truck with three enormous trays on the back. The truck driver wanted to kill Cleo to sell her for dog meat, but the circus crew was travelling the same road, moving from town to town. Mischka saw her and saved her. Now she's a circus camel. Cleo's favourite food is popcorn and her favourite pastime is doing tricks to make kids laugh. But now she's hurt and she's frightened, so we need to keep really still, really silent, while Mischka settles her down.'

'You can't...' the cop snapped, but Mathew had been deliberately lowering his voice, lower and lower, until at the end the kids were straining to hear. The cop's voice was like a staccato blast into the peace.

'Shush!' a pigtailed poppet close to Mathew scolded, and the cop looked from poppet to camel to Mathew—and, amazingly, he shushed.

His gun stayed unholstered, though.

Allie was inching towards Cleo. She was talking to her, softly whispering, growing closer, closer. Bernie was watching the cop, seeing the threat. Matt had a sudden vision of Bernie launching himself through the air at the gun, and he flinched and went right back to talking this down.

'While we wait for Mischka to calm Cleo down, maybe I should tell you about camels,' he told the kids 'Cleo's a dromedary. That means she only has one hump. Her hump's used to store energy and water, meaning she can go for days without drinking. Two-hump camels are called Bactrian camels.

They still roam wild in the deserts and mountains of Mongolia. You could ask your teachers...' he smiled at the two young women, imbuing them with more authority than they seemed to have '... to show you Mongolia on the map. Camels were brought to Australia in the olden days to help the early settlers cart goods into the outback. There are lots of stories about the pioneer camels on the Internet.'

And, just like that, he had the two trainee teachers on side. They stopped being hysterical teenagers and turned into the professionals they'd one day become.

Allie had managed to reach Cleo. She was a slip of a girl holding Cleo's halter and starting to soothe her. The cop's gun was drooping, and Mathew kept right on talking, inexorably turning a Wild Animal into Educational Opportunity.

'Camels were used extensively to open up this country,' he said. 'Cleo's mother was a wild camel, but she's descended from those first camels brought here all that time ago. When people started using trucks and trains, they let the camels loose to do what they wanted. But imagine all that time ago, girls and boys. These camels came from Pakistan. Imagine putting animals like Cleo onto boats not much bigger than the fishing schooners in our bay and bringing them all the way to Australia.'

'They would have been as scared as Cleo,' the poppet said.

'Indeed they would.' The older of the two trainee teachers finally had herself in hand, a professional in training, and, in the face of Matt's calm, she was ready to take over again. 'We'll find pictures of them on the Internet this very day, and we might start a project.' And then she looked at the cop—who still had his hand on the gun.

'Can you please put that away,' she snapped. 'The children have had enough of a fright for one day. Will the camel be okay, Miss…Miss…Mischka?'

'I think she's been shot,' Allie said and they all, without a single exception, turned to stare at the cop.

'Hey, it wasn't me…' he started but Allie shook her head.

'No,' she said soothingly. 'This is from air pellets. Someone's shot her with an air rifle.'

'And they've hurt her?' another of the kids demanded and Allie bit her lip and nodded and turned back to Cleo.

'Well,' the older of the trainees said, 'there's wickedness everywhere, isn't there, boys and girls, and yes, I saw that stone as well, Adam Winkler, and we'll be discussing it as soon as we're all inside. Which is where we're heading now. We'll leave these people to care for Cleo. Please let us know how she gets on, Miss Mischka. Thank you, Officer, for bringing us help so promptly. All right, children, right turn, quick march, back to class single file and we'll leave Cleo in peace. Let's go learn about camels.'

The girl would be a good teacher, Matt thought appreciatively. He would have watched her usher her charges and her fellow trainee back into the school, but he was too busy watching Allie.

The cop decided to guard the gate. He wasn't leaving until the school yard was cleared of camel, but he didn't want any part of persuading same camel into a trailer.

Bernie elected to watch the cop.

This was an act of sabotage and deliberate cruelty, Matt thought, as Allie settled Cleo some more. He had a clear idea now of what must have happened. The camel enclosure had been destroyed and the camels shot with air pellets to drive them crazy with pain. That there hadn't been at least one tragedy was a miracle.

'Have you had vandalism before?' he asked Allie.

'Not like this.' She was picking daisies and feeding them to Cleo. Matt made a mental note to send a gardener in to make reparation before anyone noticed. 'We have kids around the circus all the time, trying to get in to see free shows, checking out the animals, even trying to pinch things from our stalls. But this...' She looked at Cleo's flank and winced. 'Someone's come in during breakfast, which is when we have our performance meeting—it's about the only fifteen minutes in the entire twenty-four when there's no one watching. Everything's securely locked but they used bolt cutters to knock down the enclosure. Then they must have deliberately shot them to make them crazy.'

'But never before? Nothing like this?'

'No.'

She was rubbing behind the big camel's ears but the hand she used was shaking.

She was pale and growing paler.

'It didn't happen,' he said, a little too sharply, enough to make Cleo edge away a little—but Cleo had daisies now, and her own personal person and she wasn't about to tear away in fright. 'Nothing dire happened,' he said more gently. 'Pharaoh and Caesar are safe, no one's hurt and this wound on Cleo's side seems like superficial grazing. Air pellets sting, but unless they hit an eye they don't do lasting damage. I'll call the vet now.'

'The cop would have shot Cleo if you hadn't been here,' she said, just as dully. 'I should say thank you.' Then she seemed to haul herself together. She leaned into Cleo's long, soft neck and sighed. 'I do thank you. I'm so grateful.'

'It's all been a bit much to take in over twenty-four hours,' he said softly. 'I'm sorry.'

'Me, too, for all sorts of reasons.' She closed her eyes for a moment, leaned against the camel and let the warmth of the morning sun rest on her face. It was as if she was gathering strength, he thought, for when she opened her eyes again she looked different.

Moving on.

'How did you know how I found Cleo?' she demanded. 'And how did you know her mother was killed?'

He'd known because Jenny had told him while they were waiting in the wings last night, but he wasn't about to tell her that. He needed to make her smile.

'Spies,' he told her and she glanced sharply at him and saw he was trying to tease. She even managed a lopsided smile in return.

'You have spies? Bugs on the dogs?'

'On Tinkerbelle,' he said promptly. 'The tiny spot under her left ear isn't a spot at all. If you ever use flea powder we're doomed. It muffles reception no end.'

She grinned. 'Whoa, what a traitor.'

But then her smile died. It was a weird time. They were standing in the schoolyard waiting for the trailer. The sun was warm on their faces, the camel was settling, the cop was on cop duty at the gate, making sure no wild animals got out or came in, and Bernie was making sure the cop's gun stayed exactly where it belonged.

In a moment the trailer would arrive, there'd be the vet to arrange, and the circus was due to start in an hour.

In an hour this woman would be back in pink spangles, in charge of her world, but for now…she seemed bereft and alone, and once again he felt that urge to reach out and touch her.

Protect her from all-comers?

Whoa, that was a primeval urge if ever he'd felt one. This woman didn't want a knight on a white charger even if he wanted to be one.

But…

What if he saved her whole circus?

The thought was suddenly out there, front and centre. He was wealthy by anyone's standards. He could pay off debts, fund those dratted animal retirees, keep Sparkles going into perpetuity.

'Don't even think it,' she said into the stillness.

'Think what?'

'What you're thinking.'

'What am I thinking?'

'The same as I was thinking all night,' she told him. 'I'm looking at you right now and I'm seeing sympathy. I read about you on the web last night. You're not a minion in Bond's Bank—you *are* Bond's Bank. You could fund us a thousand times over. Last night I read about you and I thought this morning I'd head back to Margot's and throw myself on her neck, then get her to bully you into extending the loan.'

'She might do it, too.' He was unsure where to go with this. This wasn't your normal business discussion. This was intensely personal—and he didn't do personal. Or did he?

'I know she might,' Allie agreed. 'So I lay in bed all night and thought about it and decided I have an ageing circus with an ancient ringmaster with a heart condition. I have Bella who'll break her heart when she has to move away from the circus but she already struggles to get up and down the caravan steps and the caravans are ancient themselves. I have geriatric clowns. They're my great-uncles but I can see past that. I can see they need to retire. We have a couple of great acts but most of the circus is failing. Your news is appalling, but how much more appalling if I drag this out longer? If I plead for an extension, then it's on my head, and I can't wear it. I…can't.'

For a moment he thought she might cry, but she didn't. Instead she bit her lip, then tilted her chin and met his gaze straight on.

'The goodwill you get for selling this place, our booking rights, our name, will probably get you enough to cover our debts—apart from the animal refuge debt but I'll worry about that later. I've insisted Grandpa pay into superannuation for everyone—I assume that fund's safe?'

'It is.'

'Well, then,' she said. 'That's that. You've given us two weeks and I don't want more. You're calling in the loan and you have every right. For the next two weeks we might need you as our ring-master—and our friend—but after that…Thank you, Mr Bond, but that's all.'

CHAPTER SIX

BY THE TIME they had Cleo back at the circus, the vet was waiting. All three camels had pellet wounds. The injuries were superficial but the vet was grim-faced.

'It's a wonder these guys didn't kill themselves with fear. Someone shooting these into their flanks…I'll talk to the police. If we could find out who, we could lay charges, but I'm betting it'll be a bored teenager with a new air gun.'

But what about the fencing? Mathew thought. The bolts between the fencing had been cut with speed and precision. Surely a kid would simply aim an air gun through the wire?

Bolt cutters took strength. Adult strength. And someone must have aimed the gun from the direction of the truck, so the camels couldn't retreat.

He wanted to talk to the cop, but his experience with the town's constable wasn't encouraging.

He glanced at Allie, who was helping wash Cleo's side with disinfectant. He wasn't about to share worries about thugs with bolt cutters with Allie. She had more than enough to worry about.

But assets needed to be protected. That was a rule ingrained into his banker mind since time immemorial. These were the bank's assets, he thought, though as he looked over the wounded camels and watched the geriatric circus crew fuss around them, he thought the word asset hardly applied.

Still, he took himself out of earshot, made a couple of phone calls and felt happier. He'd have security guards here by tonight.

He turned and Allie was approaching him. She looked businesslike, and he wondered how much effort it was costing to keep herself calm in the face of the future before her. What was she proposing? To spend the rest of her life paying for the keep of geriatric animals?

'There'll be no camel show today,' she said. 'They'll need time to settle but it's fine—I'll put in an extra dog show. We'll leave the camels in view so the kids can see them as they go in and out, and we'll put up a notice saying what's happened. With a bit of luck it might even out our air gunner—there'll be kids who'll know what's happened. Mike's applying lots of bright red antiseptic so their wounds look even more dramatic than they are. Meanwhile I need to amend your cheat sheet.'

'My cheat sheet...' His mind wasn't working like it should be, or maybe he was having trouble switching from banker to outrider to teacher to...ringmaster? Or to the guy who just wanted to watch Allie.

'Your notes for tonight's performance,' she said patiently. 'Tinkerbelle and Fairy can put on an awesome act if needed and they're needed now. Okay, Maestro, time to suit up.'

'Maestro?'

'Maestro, all the way from the vast, impenetrable reaches of Outer Zukstanima,' she said and chuckled. 'It's a circus tradition. That's who we've decreed you are. By the way, when you're not in the ring can I call you Matt?'

'No!'

'I'm not calling you Mathew for two weeks,' she retorted. 'It's a banker's name. It's the same as your grandfather's, according to the website I read. So Mathew is your banking name and Maestro is your circus name. What do I call you when I just want to talk?'

There was a question to take him aback. Or, actually, just to take him back.

'Okay, Matt,' he said, before he could think any more, and it was like a window being levered, opening into the past. Matt was who he really was, in his head, but he admitted it to no one.

His memories of his big sister Lizzy were hazy, but her voice was still with him. '*Matt, come and play with me. Matt, you're messing up my painting. Mattie, hold my hand while we cross the street.*'

And his mother—also a banker...

'Elizabeth, call your brother Mathew. Mathew, call your sister Elizabeth.'

And the two of them grinning at each other and knowing that, regardless of how the world saw them, they were really Matt and Lizzy. He'd stayed Matt in his head, he thought, but only in his head. No one else ever used the diminutive.

'What did I say? What's wrong?' Allie demanded and he hauled himself back to the present with a jerk. 'I'm sorry,' she said, and she was watching his face. 'I've hurt you. The web said your family was killed. Is that what's wrong? Did they call you Matt?'

How intuitive was this woman?

'Nothing's wrong,' he said, more harshly than he intended. 'But Matt is okay.'

And suddenly it was.

For two weeks he was playing ringmaster. Make-believe. Why not extend it? For two weeks he could be Matt in his private life and he didn't have to be a banker at all.

With Allie. With The Amazing Mischka.

He should stay being a banker, he thought. He should insist that at least his name stayed the same, but Allie was moving on, and she was taking him with her. She seized his hand and tugged him forward to her grandparents' caravan, where the circus world in the form of his ringmaster's coat and hat waited.

Memories of Lizzy were suddenly all around him. 'Come on, Matt...'

The pain of knowing she wasn't there... He'd been six years old and the agony was still fresh. Lizzy.

Do not go there. Do not ever let yourself near that kind of emptiness again.

But... 'Excellent,' Allie was saying and the pressure on his hand intensified. Strong and warm—and very, very unsettling. 'Matt is nice and easy to say,' she decreed. 'And it makes you sound far less toffy. We can relax around nice, plain Matt.'

'Nice and plain? Says you who's about to force me into spangly top hat and tails.'

'There is that,' she said and she chuckled. 'Matt and Maestro seem a fearsome combination. For the next two weeks you're our hero. We'll like you in both personas, and we can forget about Mathew the Banker entirely.'

Matt or Maestro? He was thrown off balance by both. He shouldn't answer to either. He felt…he felt…

Okay, he didn't know how he felt. He had an almost overwhelming urge to head back to Margot's, climb into his gorgeous car and go home to Sydney. Taking leave had been a bad idea.

He'd done it to say goodbye to Margot but now Margot had no intention of dying, at least for the next two weeks.

If he left, would she still die?

If he left they'd have no ringmaster. And more. Allie had the weight of this whole organisation on her shoulders. How could he walk away? He couldn't walk away from Allie, he couldn't walk away from Margot, but cool, contained Mathew Bond was feeling way out of his comfort zone.

Allie left him to dress herself. He put on his uniform and stared at himself in Henry's mirror and thought…what was he doing here?

He knew what he was doing here. He had no choice.

A knock on the van door signalled Allie's return. She'd transformed into Mischka faster than he'd thought possible. How on earth had she applied those eyelashes? They were…extraordinary.

'I'm glad ringmasters don't need fake eyelashes,' he said faintly and she grinned.

'You'd look awesome. I have spares if you'd like.'

'Thank you, but no.'

'No?' She was teasing again, her sparkle returning with her spangles, and he felt like applauding the courage she was showing.

And the way she looked.

And the way she smiled…

'I'm ready,' he said, more roughly than he'd intended, and he stepped down from the van, but she didn't move back like he'd thought she would.

'The vet says you gave him your credit card details and all the veterinary costs of the camels are on you,' she said and she was still far too close.

'I…yes.' He hesitated. 'The circus is in receivership. That's what receivers do.'

'What, throw good money after bad? You realise these camels aren't worth anything? They stand up and get down and kneel, and they don't bite but there's not much else I can teach them. Saving them isn't a financial decision.'

'No,' he said and she looked up at him.

He was still too close.

She was still too close.

'So it's nothing about receivership and I do need to thank you,' she said, and suddenly the desire to reach forward and touch her was almost over-whelming.

Almost. They were in full view of the crowd assembling for the performance. Any move he made now would be a public move, and he had no intention of making a public move.

Or any move, he told himself harshly. No move at all.

'So let's get this circus moving,' she said a bit breathlessly, and her breathlessness told him she was as aware of him as he was of her—which was another reason for him to step back. And step back he did.

'Let's go show some eyelashes,' he managed.

'One set of eyelashes,' she said and grinned. 'Coward.'

'Story of my life,' he said and turned and headed for the circus.

* * *

Despite the chaos of the morning, the circus ran like well oiled clockwork. The ponies and dogs did their stuff without the camels. The act was a bit shorter than usual and not so impressive— but then Mischka moved seamlessly into a performance with just the dogs and he stopped thinking not impressive. He started thinking the opposite. Quite simply, Mischka and her two nondescript dogs left him awed.

One girl in silver sparkles, dancing, turning, tumbling. Two adoring dogs following every move.

They'd do anything for her, he thought, as he watched them from his position ringside. She wasn't feeding them, bribing them or even talking to them. She moved and they moved, like shadows beside her, in front of her, behind her, depending on her direction. She danced backward, they were up on their hind legs strutting forward. She danced forward, they did the same thing backward. She tumbled, they turned somersaults with her. She spun, they spun.

She stood on her head and they jumped across her spread legs and turned in crazy circles around her head. The crowd went wild.

She stood and bowed and the dogs bowed with

her. A camera flashed in the front row and he was momentarily distracted—no cameras were allowed and it was in the list of things he was supposed to watch for as ringmaster—but the guy put the camera away fast as soon as he saw Matt watching him, and Matt thought—why wouldn't you want to take a picture of this girl and these dogs?

'Why doesn't she put this act on all the time?' he asked Fizz as Allie and her dogs disappeared behind the curtains. Fluffy was out in the centre of the ring, setting up the next joke. Fizz and Mathew had a fraction of time to speak.

'It takes too much out of her,' Fizz said. 'That's an amazing acrobatic performance and she still has to do the trapeze act. She's so good we could just about run the circus around her only she'd fall in a heap.' He frowned then and glowered at Matt and Matt knew he wasn't Matt in this guy's eyes. He was the guy who was pulling the rug from under all of them. 'She's falling in a heap anyway. She's not eating. She's not sleeping. Her van light was on all last night, and when we bullied her to eat breakfast this morning she looked like she was going to throw up. But there's nothing we can do about it. Nothing any of us can do.'

He didn't wait for a response—maybe because he knew Matt didn't have an answer to give.

Instead he pinned on his clown grin, he bounced out to join Fluffy and the circus went on.

They took their bows as usual, they started clearing, ready for the evening performance in four hours, and at some stage Allie realised their ringmaster was no longer among them.

Fair enough, she thought as she worked on. He had his own life. He'd agreed to play ringmaster. That didn't mean he had to be hands-on, a true member of the circus troupe.

So why did she feel…empty?

No reason at all, she told herself. She had enough to worry about without Mathew…Matt Bond's continual presence. He sort of…unnerved her.

He'd kissed her.

She'd been kissed before. No big deal.

Yes, but Mathew Bond was a big deal.

'He's Matt,' she told herself and she said it out loud as if the words could somehow make him ordinary.

He wasn't ordinary.

He'd saved her camel.

He was killing her circus.

No. It wasn't him, she told herself fairly. She couldn't hold it against him. Her grandfather had killed the circus the moment he'd taken out that loan, and he'd taken out the loan because of her.

The guilt was killing her.

Everything was killing her. There were so many emotions—and overriding them all was the image of one sexy banker.

But it wasn't just that he was sexy, she thought. Yes, there was an element—or more than an element—of reaction to the fact that he was drop dead gorgeous and he had a killer smile and when he touched her, her body burned—but there was also the way he swept into the ring as if he owned it. There was the way he'd caught the children's interest today and turned kids and trainee teachers from antagonistic to gunning for Cleo all the way. There was the way he'd paid the vet's bills, which would be huge. She knew it was a small amount for him but he hadn't had to do it, and he'd smiled at her and looked worried about Cleo, and he'd stopped the cop shooting her—and then, when she'd asked about his name and he'd said Matt, he'd looked as if she'd pierced something that hurt. A lot.

There were complexities within the man and she was intrigued as well as attracted, but she'd better not be either she told herself, because being attracted to the banker was just plain dumb. Letting him kiss her had been dumb. It was the way to get her life into an even deeper mess than it already was.

'Just do what comes next,' she told herself, so she did. She finished clearing up. She had three hours before the evening performance. She checked her camels again, and then changed into respectable and went to the hospital to see Henry and Bella.

It didn't help. Her grandmother looked worse than her grandpa. It was as if everything was being taken away from her, and the only thing she had to cling to was Henry.

So what was there for Allie to cling to? she thought bleakly as she left them.

Her grey mood was threatening to overwhelm her. She had to get herself together, she told herself harshly. There was another show to put on tonight.

She was so tired all she wanted to do was crawl under a log somewhere and sleep.

She walked out of the main entrance to the hospital—and a gorgeous British Racing Green Rover was sitting in the car park. And Mathew/Matt/ Maestro, or whoever this man was, was leaning against the driver's door as if he had all the time

in the world to wait, and with one look she knew
he was waiting for her.

With her dogs?

Tinkerbelle and Fairy were in the car, their little
heads hanging out of the window, their tails wagging almost enough to vibrate the car. What on
earth were they doing here? They should be ready
for the show. She should be ready for the show.

She glanced at her watch. No, she still had two
and a half hours. She was so tired she was losing
sense of time.

'Hi,' he said as she walked—very slowly—down
the steps towards him. Her legs didn't seem like
they wanted to carry her.

'H…hi,' she ventured back.

'Fizz tells me you're not eating,' he said gently
as she reached him. 'He said you didn't eat breakfast and you hardly touched lunch. He checked the
fridge in your van and he's horrified. I've just bullied Margot into eating dinner and now it's your
turn. Hop in the car, Allie. We're going to eat.'

What could a girl do except climb into his gorgeous car and hug her ecstatic dogs and wait for
him to tell her what he was about to do with her?

How pathetic was that? But in truth Allie had

gone past pathetic. She hadn't slept. She'd spent the morning being terrified for her camels. She'd given a performance which took every ounce of energy she possessed, she'd spent time with an emotional, devastated set of grandparents, and somehow she had to gear up for another performance tonight.

If a tsunami swept inland now, she thought, she didn't have the energy to run.

She didn't want to run. She wanted to sink back into the gorgeous leather seats of Matt's fabulous car and simply stop.

He seemed to sense it. He didn't speak, just quietly climbed into the driver's seat and set the big motor purring towards the sea.

He paused at the strip of shops on the esplanade and disappeared into the fish shop. She could climb out and go home, she thought as she waited, but it'd seem ungrateful. The dogs were on her knees, and they were heavy. She didn't have the energy to push them off and, quite simply, she was past making such a decision.

Passive R Us, she thought mutely, but she didn't even begin to smile.

Mathew returned, booted the dogs into the back seat and handed her the parcel of fish and chips— a big, fat bundle of warmth. He glanced at her sharply and then nosed the car away from the shops, around the headland, away from the town.

He pulled into a reserve on the far side of the headland, by a table and benches overlooking the sea.

'Is it okay to let the dogs loose?' he asked, and she had enough energy to think thank heaven the dogs weren't white and fluffy; they were plain, scruffy brown. They could tear in crazy circles on the sand and still look presentable for the show. So that was what they did while Matt produced a tablecloth from the back of the car—linen?—plates, cutlery, napkins, glassware—and then he fetched the parcel from her knees and placed it reverently in the middle of his beautifully laid table.

'Dinner, my lady,' he intoned in the voice of Very Serious Butler, 'is served.'

The ridiculousness of the whole tableau was enough to shake her lethargy. Haziness receded. She climbed from the car and looked at the table in astonishment. The council picnic table was transformed into an elegant dining setting. Gum trees were hanging overhead, filled with corellas, vivid green and red parrots coming to perch for the night. Behind them were miles of glorious beach, no vestige of wind, the only sound being the soft hush of the surf and the calls of the sandpipers darting back and forth on the wet sand. Down on the beach Fairy and Tinkerbelle were digging their way to China in a setting that was so picturesque it took her breath away.

This was Fish and Chips with Style.

'Margot and I had a discussion,' Matt said, leading her to the table simply by taking her hand and tugging. 'Margot thought I should take you out to dinner, somewhere fancy. I thought you might like to sit on the beach. We've compromised. This is Margot's idea of picnic requirements. She can be quite insistent for someone who's almost dead.'

'She's very much alive,' Allie managed. 'Mathew, I should go back...'

'Did we agree it was Matt?'

'Nobody calls you Matt.'

'No,' he said and she couldn't figure whether there was regret there or not. No matter, he was moving on. 'But you do. Please.' He unwrapped the paper to expose slivers of golden crumbed fish fillets and gorgeous crunchy chips. He poured lemonade into the crystal glasswear.

'I know wine matches the setting,' he said. 'But you have to hang upside down tonight and I don't want you sleeping on the job.'

'No, Maestro,' she said and he chuckled.

'Excellent. Maybe I need to be Maestro tonight. The boss.' He saw her hesitation and he placed his hand on her shoulder in a fleeting gesture of reassurance. 'Allie, the circus crew knows where you are—they concur with my plan to give you a couple of hours off. They're doing everything needed so you can walk back in the gates at twenty past seven, don your false eyelashes and go straight to the ring. So you have two full hours to eat and to sleep.'

'I could go back to the circus and sleep.'

'Would you sleep?' He headed to the back of the car and hauled out a massive picnic rug and a load of cushions. 'You might nap,' he conceded, 'but you can nap here. Herewith a beach bed, my lady, for when you've polished off enough fish and chips to keep me happy.'

And then he sat beside her and ate fish and chips and looked out at the sea and he didn't say a word—and she could eat fish and chips or not—no pressure—but the pressure was insidious. The late afternoon sun was gorgeous. The dogs were deliriously happy. She was suddenly…almost happy.

It was the setting, she told herself, feeling totally

disoriented. The beach was gorgeous. The fish and chips were gorgeous.

Matt was gorgeous.

Whoa… Concentrate on fish and chips, she told herself fiercely, and don't think any further.

For gorgeous was scary.

Once Allie had disposed of enough food to satisfy him—which was a lot—Matt once again refused her a choice. He pointed to the rug and the pillows and he gave his orders.

'Lie. Sleep.'

'I can't just lie out here in public…'

'Why not? The sun's great. No one's around. I'm not asking you to sunbathe naked.'

'No,' she said and looked doubtfully at the cushions. They did look great. The dogs had already settled amongst them but Matt had ordered them to the edge so there was more than enough room for her.

She *was* tired.

'So you're standing over me to keep guard,' she said nervously and he shook his head.

'I'm on washing-up duty,' he said and proceeded to toss the remaining chips to a hundred seagulls who'd magically appeared and then bundle all the picnic gear into his capacious basket. 'That's that. And then, if you don't mind, I'll share your very big blanket.'

'You want to share my bed?'

'My nefarious plan's uncovered,' he said and gave an evil chuckle and she had to smile.

This man was an enigma. Solitary, aloof, ruthless, kind…

Mind-blowingly sexy.

She should argue, but the sun was on her face and she was full of fish and chips and her dogs were here, which made it seem…okay…and those cushions… And this man…

She slid down onto the rug and sank into the pillows and it was like she was letting go.

It wasn't just today that had exhausted her, she thought. It was…life. Matt was right; this circus was unviable. Even without the massive debt for the animals, she'd been struggling.

She'd been struggling for years. Her grandparents were growing increasingly frail. Slowly, imperceptibly, she'd taken over their roles, taking the day-to-day running of the circus onto her shoulders. As more of the performers grew older she'd simply taken on more.

But she couldn't think of that now. She couldn't

think past the pillows. All roads led to this place, she thought. All paths led to these pillows, and to this man standing over her simply assuming control.

'It's scary having you hover,' she complained and he grinned and sank down to join her. To sleep with her? Sleep in the real sense, she thought. There was no way she was up for a spot of seduction now.

'I'm only doing this to make you feel better,' he said. 'So you won't feel self-conscious snoozing alone.'

'I don't think I'll snooze.'

'Close your eyes then,' he said. 'Think of anything you like except money and circuses and grandparents and camels.'

'Is this the advice you give to all your clients?'

'Clients?'

'You are my banker,' she said and then caught herself. 'I mean, my grandparents' banker. Mathew who's really Matt.' And then she said sleepily, into her pillows, 'Why did you look upset when you told me you were Matt? Why does no one call you Matt? Is it about your family?'

He'd lain beside her, feeling vaguely self conscious but knowing he needed to do this to make her relax. There was a good foot between them. The dogs were on the end of the rug. This could be totally impersonal.

It wasn't. It was as if there was a cocoon around them, enclosing them in a bubble of space where there could be no secrets.

It was an illusion, Matt thought, but even so, a question which would normally make him freeze was suddenly able to be answered.

'My grandfather was Mathew,' he said. 'My father was Mathew. My great-grandfather was Mathew. I expect if ever I have a son he'll be Mathew.'

'That doesn't leave much room for the imagination,' she said sleepily. 'But…Matt?'

'My father and my grandfather were…to put it bluntly…strong personalities, and my mother was just as rigid,' he said. 'You've met my great-aunt. Picture her multiplied by a hundred. Even Margot would never consider calling me Matt.'

'But someone did.'

'My sister Lizzy,' he said. 'Elizabeth. As the biography you read told you, she died when I was six, in a car crash with my parents. Matt died with her.'

'I'm so sorry,' she whispered. 'Oh, Matt…'

'It's a long time ago,' he said, more roughly than he intended. 'After the crash my grandfather was even more formal. There was no nonsense about him, no emotion, no stupid diminutives. I didn't want a diminutive anyway.'

'But you think of yourself as Matt.'

He started to say no. He started—and then he stopped.

He did, he conceded. On the surface and all through the exterior layers he was Mathew, but underneath was where the pain lay. To let anyone call him Matt...

'Does me calling you Matt hurt?'

Yes, he thought. It was like biting on a tooth he knew was broken. But he glanced at her, lying sideways on her cushion, drifting towards sleep, and he knew that somehow she was worth the pain.

Something in this girl was inching through the layers of armour he'd built. He knew pain would come, but for now all he felt was a gentle, insidious warmth.

He hadn't felt cold, he thought. He hadn't thought he wanted...

He didn't want. This woman was a bereft client of the bank, and he needed to remember it.

He needed to put things back on a business foot-ing, fast.

So talk about her business affairs now?

No. He might be a businessman but he wasn't cruel. He'd brought her here—wise or not—to give her time out and he'd follow through. He'd let her sleep.

But first... She'd exposed part of him he didn't want exposed. Fair was fair.

'How about you?' he asked. 'Who called you Allie?'

'My mother, of course,' she said, but she didn't stir. There didn't seem any pain there.

'But I gather you've been cared for by your grandparents since you were tiny.'

'You have been doing your research.' She snug-gled further into the pillows. Tinkerbelle, or maybe it was Fairy, one of the identical dogs with iden-tical tails that whirred like helicopters when they were happy, which would be now, had snuggled onto the pillow beside her and she held her close. 'Gran and Grandpa have been great. I had the best childhood.'

'Without a mum?'

'I know, sometimes I feel guilty for thinking it,' she said. 'Mum took off with the circus fire-eater when I was two. She and Scorcher left for a bigger, better circus where they could make more money, but it didn't last. Scorcher went on to make his fortune in America and we haven't heard from him since. Mum moved on to a series of men, places, adventures. She's currently working as a psychic, reading Tarot cards up on the Gold Coast. She sends me Christmas and birthday cards. Every now and then she whirls in, usually needing money, spins our life into confusion and spins out again. I've figured she does love me, as much as she's able to love anyone, but I'm eternally grateful she and Scorcher left me behind. My family is this circus. Gran and Grandpa, Fizz and Fluffy, the crew, the animals; they've been here all my life. Sparkles is my family.' She sighed then and buried her face in her pillow, so her next words were muffled. 'For two more weeks.'

Matt thought back to the instructions he'd left at head office. Feelers had been put out already. There were circuses—one in particular—hovering, wanting to cherry pick the best of this little outfit. Their bookings. The best of their performers.

The circus was in receivership, like it or not, and instructions were to sell.

'If you wanted you could stay on in the circus,' he said tentatively. 'There are bigger commercially viable outfits that would be very willing to take you on. Your acts are wonderful.'

'But just me,' she said softly and hugged her dog closer. 'By myself. How lonely would that be? As I said, we're family. We'll stay together. I'm not sure about the elephants, though.'

'Let me help,' he said, and he hadn't known he was going to say it until he did. 'Maybe I can take on the retired elephant fund.'

She rolled over then and looked at him—really looked at him. It seemed weirdly intimate. Girl lying on pillows, the sinking sun on her face, her dog snuggled against her. Her banker sitting above her, offering...finance?

'Why would you do that?'

'I like elephants?'

She smiled then, almost a chuckle, but her smile faded.

'No,' she said. 'Um...not. Years ago my grandfather asked a favour of Bond's Bank and it put us into all sorts of bother. I think it's time for the... bonds...to be cut.'

'And the elephants?'

'I've already started contacting welfare groups. I'll find somewhere.'

'Not as good as where they are now.'

'No,' she said softly. 'But that goes for all of us.' She sighed, snuggled even further into the pillows and closed her eyes. 'Nowhere's as good as where I am right this minute,' she said softly. 'Nowhere at all, so if you don't mind, I might just go to sleep and enjoy it.'

She slept.

He watched over her.

It was a curious sensation, sitting on the grassy verge above a deserted beach, watching the sandpipers scuttle to collect the detritus of an outgoing tide—and watching a lady sleep.

He felt absurdly protective. More, he felt…emotional. As if he'd do anything to protect her.

In days of old, when knights were bold...

There was a romantic notion, he told himself, and the thought of himself as knight on white charger almost made him smile.

But not quite, for the notion wouldn't go away. Something in this woman stirred him as he'd never been stirred.

It was because she was needy, he told himself. She needed protection.

But was she needy? She was a feisty, courageous, multi-talented circus performer and accountant, and she'd just knocked back his offer to help.

He was her banker.

He didn't want to be her banker.

Where were his thoughts taking him? Were they turning him into Matt?

Exposing him?

What if...? he thought. What if...?

She looked so vulnerable. She *was* so vulnerable. He could pick her up, he thought, and take her back to Sydney and keep her safe.

Yeah, that was white charger territory again, he thought ruefully. Romantic stuff. He had a very large apartment looking over the harbour. Even so, it'd hardly house Gran and Grandpa and Fizz and Fluffy and Tinkerbelle and Fairy and three ruddy great camels...

He did grin then, thinking of the concierge of his apartment block. Thinking of camels.

Then he glanced down at Allie again and he stopped thinking of concierge or camels.

What he wanted, he decided, more than anything else in the world, was to sink onto the pillows, gather her into his arms and hold her.

But even in sleep he could see her fierce independence. It was engendered by her background, he thought. He knew enough of the back story of this circus now to have a good idea of its dynamics.

Yes, the circus had raised her, but it hadn't been long before Allie had more or less taken over. Everyone his people had talked to when researching the circus had referred to Allie. 'Allie only hires the best. Allie keeps the best animal quarters. Allie's safety standards are second to none.'

This circus…Allie's family… Allie's life.

It wasn't possible to keep it going. He'd looked long and hard at the figures. Even without that appalling pension fund for retired animals, the performers were ageing, the superstructure needed major refurbishment and the whole organisation was winding down.

But she'd fight for what she had left, he thought. He could see her on this farmlet she dreamed of but it wasn't a dream he was seeing. It was a nightmare. One girl working her heart out to provide for the remnants of a finished circus.

That was why he was feeling protective?

That was why he was feeling cracks in his armour?

He needed to get a grip. He was her banker, nothing else.

Except for the next two weeks he was her ring-master.

'Yes, but that's all,' he said aloud and Allie stirred in her sleep and he felt...he felt...

As if he needed to head along the beach and walk, or maybe run. He needed to get rid of this energy, get rid of this weird jumble of heart versus head.

The dogs looked up at him, questioning.

'You guys stay here,' he told them. 'I'm not going far. You're in protection mode.'

They snuggled down again as if they agreed.

He walked but not out of sight. His jumble of thoughts refused to untangle.

He was in protection mode as well, whether Allie wanted it or not.

Whether he wanted it or not.

'Matt,' he said out loud and the sound of the name he hadn't used for years startled him. 'Matt.'

Put the armour back on, he told himself harshly. Turn yourself back into Mathew.

The problem was...what?

He glanced up the beach, to the sleeping woman with her huddle of protective dogs and he thought…

He thought the problem was that he didn't know how to turn back into what he'd been. Mathew seemed to be crumbling.

He'd get himself back together, he told himself, after two weeks as ringmaster. Two weeks as knight on white charger?

She doesn't want me to be knight on white charger, he told himself and hurled a few pebbles into the sea and tried to figure what he wanted.

Sydney. The bank. Normality.

Yeah? He glanced back at the sleeping girl and normality seemed a million miles away.

CHAPTER SEVEN

TWO HOURS LATER he dropped Allie back at the circus. She'd woken subdued. They'd driven back in near silence. She'd hesitated before she left the car but in the end she'd said a simple thank you. Then she'd paused. A guy in a security uniform was standing by the gate.

'You are?' she'd said while Matt waited.

'From Bond's Security,' the man said. 'We have security covered.'

She looked back at Matt, and then she sighed.

'You're taking care of your own?'

'Yes,' he said because there was nothing else to say, and she gave an almost imperceptible nod and disappeared back into a life that was almost over.

He had half an hour to evening performance. He needed to go back to Margot's to put his good trousers and white shirt on so he could don his ringmaster apparel over the top.

He walked in the front door and Margot was bundled up like a snow bunny: two coats, fur boots, mittens, fur hat and rug.

'It's um…summer, Margot,' he said and she snorted.

'Says you who have body fat.' Then she paused and looked at him critically. 'Body mass, I should say. Muscle. You look like you could be Allie's catcher.'

'Rather Valentino than me,' he said, suppressing a shudder. It was the one part of the circus he didn't enjoy—watching Allie fly through the air, totally dependent on a great bull of a man whose grip was like iron but whose intelligence…

'He hasn't dropped her yet,' Margot said gently, watching his face. 'So I can't see why he would tonight. Come on then, get changed. I don't want to miss anything.'

'You're coming?'

'Yes. Hurry up.'

'They can hardly start without the ringmaster,' he said dryly and she cast him a sharp look.

'Neither they can,' she said softly. 'How fortunate.'

Things went well that night. Allie's dog routine was even more spectacular—their time on the beach seemed to have done them good. No one dropped anything or was dropped. The audience roared when they were supposed to roar and they hushed when they were supposed to hush.

Margot had an awesome seat. Tickets had been sold out for days but Allie saw her arrive and some-one ran for a chair and she was placed right up the front, supervising all.

Matt was aware of her as he worked.

She was a force to be reckoned with, his Aunt Margot. He knew she disapproved of the way he'd been raised. She'd never criticised his grandfather to him, but he'd overheard a couple of heated conversations with his grandfather. Very heated.

'You're bringing that boy up to be a financial calculator, not a child,' she'd told her brother. *'For heaven's sake, give him some freedom.'*

Margot was a Bond—stern, unyielding, undemonstrative—yet she'd never had anything to do with the bank. She'd lived on her own income. She'd refused family help. She was an independent spirit. So maybe a part of her wasn't a Bond.

A true Bond would choke seeing Mathew Bond in glittery top hat and tails, Matt thought, but Margot cheered and gasped with the rest of them, and at the end of the performance he watched Allie

rush around to talk to her and, to his astonishment, he saw his normally undemonstrative aunt
give Allie a hug.

As the big top emptied he strolled across to join
them. Casually. As if it didn't do anything to his
head to see these two women together. Allie was
kneeling beside Margot's chair, smiling and holding her hand, her affection obvious, and the old
woman, who only days ago had decreed she was
dying, was holding her hand back and smiling and
chuckling at something Allie was saying.

He'd given the circus a two-week reprieve, he
thought, but it had also given Margot two weeks.

And after two weeks?

Worry about that then, he told himself. Maybe
he could pick Margot up and forcibly take her back
to Sydney...

Yeah. She'd be about as at home in his Sydney
apartment as Allie's camels would be.

The women broke apart as he approached, both
looking at him critically. Banker in spangles. He
could see a twinkle in Margot's eyes and half of
him loved seeing mischief again, and the other half
thought—uh oh.

'You look splendid,' Margot declared. 'And you

make a wonderful ringmaster. I just wish your grandfather was alive to see it.'

'He'll be rolling in his grave right now,' he said, smiling down at her. He loved this old lady and, no matter what, these two weeks were a gift. 'The whole Bond dynasty will be. My father, my grandfather and his grandfather before them. What do you reckon, Margot—should I give up banking and run away with the circus?'

'There's not a lot of money in circusing,' Allie said, smiling but rueful. 'Plus you'll have to look for another circus.'

'I don't know why this one's closing.' Margot suddenly sounded fretful. 'Mathew, you should buy it. You're rich enough to buy it. He is, you know,' she said to Allie, as if Matt was suddenly not there. 'Rich as Croesus. He's rolling in banking money like his father and his grandfather and great-grandfather before him. Not that it's made any of them happy. Mathew, buy a circus and have some fun.'

Allie's smile remained but it started to look fixed.

'It wouldn't work,' she said softly. 'Thank you for offering,' she told Margot, with only a sideways glance at Matt. 'But, even though this has been an appalling shock and we're not as prepared as I thought we were, this is a circus on its last legs. Look round, Margot. Half our crew is geriatric.'

'They don't look geriatric to me,' Margot snapped.

'You're how old?' Allie said and her smile returned. 'Get real, Margot. Could you manage a trapeze or two? There's a time to move on.'

'Exactly,' Margot said and glared at her nephew. 'That's what I've been telling Mathew.'

'I don't mean dying,' Allie said indignantly. 'Just...not playing with the circus any more. Taking life seriously.'

'Why don't you mean dying then?' Margot said morosely. 'You can't get any more serious than that.'

'Margot...'

'Don't you worry about me, girl,' Margot ordered with a decisive nod. 'Tell me, are you making plans to see these elephants of yours? Mathew tells me you didn't even know where they were.'

'I can't worry about them now. I'll figure...'

'You loved them,' Margot snapped. 'That's why your grandfather asked for my help in the first place. I know he told you he'd sold them to a zoo in Western Australia. I always thought it was stupid, lying to you, but now you know they're local, you could go see them. Mathew could take you.'

And the mischief was back, just like that.

'Where are they?' Allie said cautiously.

'It's an open range sanctuary, part of a farm, only it's not open to the public. You'll need to get more details from Henry but, as far as I can remember, it's on the other side of Wagga.'

'Wagga,' Allie said faintly. 'That's almost three hundred miles.'

'Matt has a nice car.' Margot sounded oblivious to a minor hiccup like three hundred miles. 'The circus doesn't do a matinee on Wednesday. You could be there and back by the evening show.'

'Not even for my elephants,' Allie said, and Matt realised there'd been a faint sheen of hope in her eyes, a lifting of the bleak acceptance he'd seen too much of, but she extinguished the hope fast now and moved on. 'Three hundred miles and back in a day with a show afterwards? That's impossible. When…when we're wound up, there'll be all the time in the world to go look at elephants.'

'But you'd like to,' Matt said slowly, watching her face.

'You have a gorgeous car,' she told him. 'But not

that gorgeous. A six hundred mile round trip? Get real. Did you like the show, Margot?'

'I loved it,' Margot said soundly.

'Well, that's all that matters,' Allie decreed. 'Keeping the punters happy. For the next two weeks this circus is going to run like clockwork, and then I'll worry about my elephants. I'll have time then.'

'In between finding houses, settling geriatric circus staff, finding a job…' Matt growled, but she shook her head. She looked fabulous, he thought, in her gorgeous pink and silver body-suit. She looked trim, taut and so sexy she took a man's breath away. She also looked desolate. But, desolate or not, she also looked strong. She was cutting him out of this equation.

'That's not your problem,' she told him. 'Margot, your nephew very kindly gave me time out today—he fed me fish and chips and he gave me time for a snooze. So he's being our ringmaster and he's being kind, but apart from that…I need to cope with this on my own.'

She'd been kneeling beside Margot. Now she rose. Matt held out his hand to help her but she ignored it.

'I do need to do this on my own,' she said, gently

but implacably. 'And I will. Thank you for your help, Mathew, and thank you for your friendship, Margot, but I need to go help pack up now. Mathew, you need to take your aunt home.'

Mathew.

My name is Matt, Matt thought, but he didn't say it. Allie was resetting boundaries, and what right did he have to step over them?

'She really wants to see those elephants.'

Settled into his car, Margot was quietly thoughtful. They were halfway home before she finally came out with what was bothering her.

'I know she does,' Matt said. 'But a six hundred mile round trip in a day is ridiculous.'

'Since when did a little matter of six hundred miles ever get in the way of a Bond?' Margot snapped, and he glanced at her and thought she looked exhausted.

How much had tonight taken out of her?

She'd turned away and was looking out of the window, over the bay to the twinkling lights of the boats at swing moorings.

'You know, it doesn't happen all that often,' she said softly into the night, and he had a feeling she was half talking to herself.

'What doesn't happen?'

She was silent for a moment. A long moment. Then…

'I fell in love,' she said at last, into the silence. 'You've seen his photograph on my mantel. Raymond. He was a lovely, laughing fisherman. He was…wonderful. But my parents disapproved— oh, how they disapproved. A Bond, marrying a fisherman. We'd come down here for a family holiday and the thought that I could meet and fall in love with someone who was so out of our world… It was insupportable—and I was insistent but not insistent enough.'

'You told him you'd marry him.'

'Yes,' she said, and her voice was suddenly bleak. She stared down at her gnarled old hand, to the modest diamond ring that had been there for as long as Matt could remember. 'We met just as the war started. I met him on the esplanade. The heel had come off my shoe and he helped me home. We went to two dances and two showings of the same picture. Then Father got wind of it and I was whisked back to Sydney. Soon afterwards, Raymond was called up and sent abroad. We wrote, though. I still have his letters. Lovely, lovely letters. Then, two years later, he came home—for a whole three weeks. He'd been wounded—he was home on leave before being sent abroad again. He came to Sydney to find me and he gave me this ring.'

She stared down at the ring and it was as if she was looking into the very centre of the diamond. Seeing what was inside. Seeing what was in her heart all those years ago.

'He wanted to marry me before he went back,' she whispered. 'And I wanted to. But my father... your great-grandfather...' She shook her head. 'He was so angry. He asked how I could know after such a short time? He said if we really loved each other it'd stand separation. He said...*I forbid it.* And I was stupid enough, dumb enough, weak enough to agree. So I kissed my Raymond good-bye and he died six months later.'

She stared down at the tiny diamond and she shook her head, her grief still raw and obvious after how many years? And then she glared straight at Matt.

'And here you are, looking at someone who's right in front of you,' she snapped. 'Allie's perfect. You know she is. I can see that you're feeling ex-actly what I was feeling all those awful, wasted years ago and you won't even put the lady in your car and go visit some elephants!'

At the end she was practically booming—and then she burst into tears.

In all the time he'd known her he'd never seen Margot cry.

Bonds didn't do emotion.

He'd seen the engagement ring on her finger. He'd never been brave enough to ask her about it. Once he'd asked his grandfather.

'A war thing,' his grandfather had snapped. *'Stupid, emotional whim. Lots of women lost their partners during the war—Margot was one of the lucky ones. At least she didn't get married and have children.'*

One of the lucky ones...

He hugged Margot now and found her a handkerchief and watched as she sniffed and sniffed again, and then she harrumphed and pulled herself together and told him to drive on—and he thought of those words.

One of the lucky ones...

A six hundred mile round trip.

Allie.

'You can do it if you want to,' Margot muttered as he helped her out of the car, and he helped her inside, he made her cocoa, helped her to bed—and then he went for a very long walk on the beach.

A six hundred mile round trip.

Allie.

Elephants.

One of the lucky ones...

Wednesday morning.

Allie had plans for this morning, but none of them were good. She had a list from the realtors of all the farmlets that were available for rent in the district in her price range. She'd added combined pensions plus what she could feasibly earn as a bookkeeper minus what it'd cost to keep the animals and it wasn't looking pretty. The places looked almost derelict.

She thought of the lovely beachside cottage Henry and Bella had told her they were paying off, and she felt ill.

They'd done this for her.

Henry was being released from hospital tomorrow. They'd kept him in until he was over his virus, but she suspected the kindly staff of the small district hospital were also giving them a break. Tomorrow they'd be back in their caravan and they'd have to face their future.

Maybe one of these properties was better than it looked in the brochure, she thought grimly. Ha.

Deeply unsettled, she fed the animals early, then took the dogs for a long walk on the deserted beach. As she walked back to the circus a helicopter was coming into land on the foreshore.

'Bond's Bank' was emblazoned on the side.

Why?

Maybe this was Matt's…Mathew's staff, she corrected herself. He'd said the circus could operate for two weeks but she was under no illusion. The circus belonged to him, lock, stock and barrel, and if he'd brought in a team to pull it apart…

She felt sick.

She stood back and watched as the chopper came to rest, as the rotor blades stopped spinning.

It was a very small chopper for a team of financiers.

Who was she kidding? she thought ruefully. Sparkles was a very small circus. Why would they need a team?

But this small? Only one guy climbed from the chopper and that was the pilot.

This had nothing to do with her, she told herself grimly.

She walked back to the circus, giving the headland and the chopper a wide berth. She walked into the circus enclosure and Matt...Mathew...was waiting for her. Casually dressed. Smiling at her with a smile that could make a girl's heart do back-flips if a girl's heart was permitted.

Which it wasn't.

She loosened the dogs' leads and the dogs raced to greet him, jumping and yelping as if he was part of the family.

Which he wasn't. He was Mathew.

'Back,' she said to the dogs, but they uncharacteristically ignored her. Maybe because Matt... Mathew...had knelt and was scratching them behind their ears and they were lick-spitting, traitorous hounds and they didn't know this guy was taking away their lifestyle and they didn't know this guy was capable of taking away their mistress's heart...

Only that was a dumb thing to think. She pinned on a smile and moved forward to greet him with what she hoped was dignified courtesy.

'Good morning.'

'Good morning yourself,' he said and straightened and smiled some more and her heart did do that stupid back-flip she'd been telling it not to. 'It's a great day for elephant visiting,' he added.

'Pardon?'

'We have a chopper,' he said. 'An hour there, an hour back, a couple of hours visiting… You'll even have time for a wee nap before evening performance.'

'What…?'

'You might need a sweater,' he said. 'It gets a bit breezy in the chopper. And elephant snacks? What do you take to an elephant you haven't seen for years?'

'I…'

'Just do it,' he said gently. 'You know you want to. Your financial adviser says this is a good idea, so who are you to argue?'

He was serious. The chopper was for elephant visiting. Not only had Matt organised for it to be delivered, it seemed he was flying.

'I've had my licence for years,' he told her cheerfully. 'Joe's spending the day on the beach while I take over his machine. It's economical,' he said as she opened her mouth to protest—if she could think of the words she needed, which she couldn't. 'Two people instead of three. Lots of fuel saved. And don't tell me I don't need to come—Bond's Bank has been financing these elephants for years, and I have a vested interest in inspecting our investment.'

And here was Bella, walking towards her, carrying her jacket. Bella, who spent every waking moment with Henry.

Had Matt lined this up with her Gran? Obviously yes.

'Matt says he'll take Henry and me to see them when Henry's well,' Bella told her, beaming. 'But just knowing you're visiting them today will do your Grandpa good. Give them our love.' And she placed a paper bag into Allie's limp hand. 'Doughnuts,' she said. 'They're very bad but Maisie and Minnie both love them. Sneak them some when no one's looking.'

Maisie and Minnie. Mother and daughter, great, lumbering Asian elephants, third and fourth generation circus bred, docile and wonderful. Allie had loved them with all her teenage heart, and that was what this mess was about. She'd fought for them.

If she climbed into the chopper with Matt, she could see them in an hour.

But what if…and she should…and it wasn't…

She had all sorts of protests and not one would come out.

Bella took the two dogs' leads. 'Come on, guys,

your mistress is visiting past loves today,' she said as Matt propelled Allie towards the chopper and Allie let herself be propelled because there didn't seem any alternative. And Matt was large and commanding and he had everything sorted and she thought, just for a moment, wouldn't it be great to put this whole mess in Matt's hands and let him sort it out?

There was a dumb thought. Her mess was nothing to do with him—she'd told him that and she was right.

But right now?

Right now she was going to see some friends she hadn't seen for years.

Where had her grandfather sent them?

Somewhere good, she pleaded silently. Somewhere to make this sacrifice worthwhile.

'Let's go,' Matt said and he helped her into the cockpit.

She sat passive as he adjusted her harness and her headphones and closed her door.

She sat passive as he slid behind the controls, did what he needed to and lifted the chopper from the ground.

She glanced across at Matt and she saw that

he was smiling, that faint devil-behind-the-smile glimmer she was starting to know.

It was a smile that made her feel being passive was her only protection.

CHAPTER EIGHT

THE JOB DESCRIPTION for a circus performer didn't come with the label big earner, so a one-time commercial flight from Sydney to Melbourne was the sum total of Allie's air travel. She'd never been in a helicopter.

Now she was in a tiny cockpit beside Matt, the cockpit seemed almost a transparent bubble, and she felt like...

She was flying?

She *was* flying, she told herself, trying hard not to cling to the edge of her seat and whimper. The chopper rose with a speed that took her breath away. She was in a bubble heading for the clouds.

She forgot to breathe.

Fort Neptune grew smaller and smaller. She was in a bubble in the sky with Matt Bond.

The floor beneath her was transparent. She could see miles of coastline falling away beneath her. She could see the Blue Mountains.

'It's safe,' Matt said through her headphones and

she tried really hard to catch her breath and act cool and toss him a look of insouciance.

'I'm just…' She saw where he was looking and carefully unfastened her white knuckles from the seat. 'It's just I'm always wary of inexperienced drivers.'

'That would be pilots.'

'Pilots,' she snapped.

'I'm very experienced.'

'You didn't hand me your CV as you got in the driver's seat,' she managed as the Blue Mountains loomed and the chopper started to rise even further. 'I like first-hand knowledge of my…chauffeur.'

'You want to radio for a reference?' he asked. He grinned and she knew, she just knew, that if she took him up on his offer she'd radio and someone would tell her that this man was competent, no, more than competent, an expert, experienced, calm and safe.

Safe.

See, that was half the problem. He didn't make her feel safe. Okay, maybe his piloting skills weren't the issue. Flying above the Blue Mountains in a transparent bubble might make her feel unsafe with anyone, but she was settling, getting used to the machine, starting to be entranced by the landscape beneath—but underlying everything was the way this man made her feel.

Unsafe?

Just unsteady, she told herself and that was reasonable. He'd pulled the rug from under the circus she loved.

No. He hadn't done that. Her grandfather had done it by taking out such a huge loan. Matt had every right to call it in.

And the unsafe bit wasn't about the loan, either, she conceded. She sneaked a quick glance across at him. He was focused again on the country ahead. He looked calm, steady, in control, and she thought—that's what the problem is.

He's more in control of my world than I am.

Concentrate on the view, she told herself. On the scenery.

And on what was waiting to meet her?

'Do…do these people know I'm coming?'

'The park's owners? Jack and Myra. Yes, they do. They're good people.'

'How do you know?'

'We do thorough research before we foreclose,' he said gently. 'We wanted to know where our money was—whether there was any chance of us retrieving it. There's not. Every cent your grandpa paid has been long spent. Jack and Myra are in trouble themselves, but not from mismanagement. It's because they care too much.'

'I'll pay them back,' she said tightly.

'With a bookkeeper's salary?' He sounded amused and she winced. She thought about the amount she was likely to earn and the amount she owed and she could see why he was amused.

And she thought again... He's more in control of my world than I am.

'Don't worry about it today,' Matt said gently. 'Today's not for finance. Today's for seeing your friends again.'

He focused on the machine again, on the myriad of instruments, on the scene ahead, and she thought—he's letting me be. Like the picnic on the beach...he's giving me space.

She felt, suddenly, stupidly, dangerously, close to tears.

This man was in control and she wasn't. She had to be.

The majestic line of the Blue Mountains was receding now, opening to the vast tracts of grassland that grew inland for hundreds of miles, spreading until they gave way to the true Australian outback.

What a place to keep retired circus animals!

'They keep all sorts,' Matt said, and it seemed he was almost following her thoughts. 'It started forty years ago when a grazier called Jack met a circus performer called Myra. Myra was a trapeze artist like you. Jack asked Myra to marry him but Myra wouldn't leave the bear the circus had owned for ten years. So Jack married Myra and Jack's farm has been home to aged circus animals ever since. They've fought to keep it going, but finally they've lost.'

So any thought of asking—begging—them to keep the elephants on for free was out of the question, Allie thought miserably, but, as she thought it, Matt's hand closed over hers. Firm, warm and strong.

'Friends today,' he repeated softly. 'Finance tomorrow.'

Surely only in Australia could such an area be one farm. Jack and Myra's holding was vast. They circled before they landed. Allie saw a vast undulating landscape with scattered bushland, big dams, a creek running through its centre, beef cattle grazing lazily in the sun—and the odd giraffe and elephant.

It was so incongruous she had to blink to believe she was seeing it.

Jack came forward to greet them as the chopper landed, elderly, lean, weathered, taciturn. He gripped Allie's hand. 'Myra's feeling a bit frail. Sorry, it'll be only me doing the tour.'

She owed this man so much money. That Jack and Myra hadn't been paid...

'I'm so sorry,' she started but Jack's hand gripped hers and held.

'You're Allie,' he said. 'We know why your animals came to us. Myra's loved you even though she's never met you. Your animals have had ten years of good living, thanks to you. You tried your best, girl, as did your grandpa, and there's no grudges. Want to meet them?' He motioned towards an ancient mud-spattered truck. 'Let's go.'

'Yes, please.' Friends today, she thought as she glanced at Matt and he smiled and ushered her towards the truck. Problems tomorrow.

And two minutes later, there they were, beside the dusty dam where two elephants soaked up the morning sun.

They were together as they always had been, two elephants lazing by the bank of a vast man-made dam, half a mile from the homestead. Minnie was

still smaller than her mother. She declined to rise
from reclining on the mud bank, but Maisie started
lumbering across to meet them.

Jack climbed out of the truck and called. Maisie
reached Jack, touched him with her great trunk—
and then her small eyes moved to see who was ac-
companying him.

Allie was out of the truck. Maisie and Minnie.
Friends.

And Maisie reacted. Her trunk came out and
touched Allie—just touched—a feather-touch on
the face as though exploring, confirming what
she'd suspected.

And it was all Allie could do not to burst into
tears.

These guys had been her friends. She'd been the
only kid in the circus, home schooled, isolated.
Her dogs were with her always, but these two…
She'd told them her problems and they'd listened;
she thought they'd understood. At fifteen, sixteen,
seventeen she hadn't been able to bear the chains
around their great stumps of legs. She'd made such
a fuss that her grandfather had mortgaged everything.

It didn't matter now. She leant all her weight
against Maisie's trunk and Maisie supported her

and she thought she'd do it again. Whatever the cost. She'd have no choice.

'The…the lions?' she managed. 'And the monkeys?'

'They're a bit more closely contained,' Jack said ruefully. 'I can't give them a hundred miles to roam, much as we'd like to. They only have a couple of miles we can fence securely.'

A couple of miles. She thought back to the six foot by ten foot cages and she thought…she thought…

She thought she just might finally burst into tears.

He stood his distance and watched.

That these elephants knew this woman had never been in doubt. They seemed to be as pleased to see her as she was to see them—that was if he was reading elephant language right which, he had to admit, was a bit of a long call. But Allie surely knew them. She was between the two elephants, hugging as much as she could of them, looking close to tears.

Maisie, the biggest of the two, lifted her left foreleg and trunk. It was a gesture that even Matt could tell was an invitation that had long been used, for

Allie accepted almost before the leg was completely raised. She swung herself up on the great raised leg, she held the trunk and the next minute she was on Maisie's back, leaning forward, hugging as much of Maisie as she could.

'Well, I never,' Jack said placidly, almost to himself. Then the old farmer grinned. 'We have ten of 'em, you know. From the moment they get here we forget they're circus animals—there's no balancing on stools here. They're as wild as we can make 'em. Some we can hardly get near any more—they're the ones that've been mistreated—but these two always like company. We figured they've been treated as right as circus animals ever can be, and their reaction confirms it.'

'We had the best act,' Allie called down to them, still elephant hugging. 'I wonder...you want to see?'

'No stools,' Jack said, and Allie grinned.

'Nope.' She stood up. She was wearing soft, clinging leggings, a baggy jacket and trainers. She tugged off her trainers and tossed them down to Matt, and her jacket followed suit.

She was left in leggings, a close fitting T-shirt and bare feet.

'Let's see if we remember,' she muttered and

now she was talking to Maisie—and to Minnie. 'Oi,' she called to Minnie. 'Oi, oi, oi. Top and tail.'

And astonishingly, ponderously, top and tail was just what happened. Minnie had risen to stand by Maisie. Now she shifted to stand close behind her mother, so close they were touching, and she took her mother's tail in her trunk and held on.

As if on cue, Allie slid over Minnie's head, onto Minnie's slightly smaller back. Then she stood, steadied, measured the distance with her eyes— then flipped into a high, tumbling somersault, high over the gap, landing flawlessly, sliding to a sitting position so Maisie didn't get the jarring shock of two feet landing on her.

And as she slid down, Maisie lifted her trunk and trumpeted, as if in triumph, and turned with the girl still on her back and headed straight into the dam.

Matt made an involuntary step forward but Jack gripped his shoulder and held. He was chuckling out loud.

'Let 'em be,' he told her. 'Maisie loves her waterhole like life itself, and she's showing off—and you think your girl wants to get off?'

She didn't. Allie was laughing with incredulous delight as Maisie stomped deep down, neck-deep into the dust-brown waterhole. Minnie lifted her trunk and trumpeted like her mother—and went right in after.

Two elephants, one waterhole, one ecstatic girl. Maisie was lowering her trunk in and out of the water, splashing like a two-year-old in the bath. Allie was under a shower to end all showers.

'I've seen this before,' Jack said in satisfaction. 'There's a bond between elephant and keeper. We've had these two for ten years now but this girl's been an important part of their lives for a long time.'

He couldn't keep his eyes from her. She was drenched, covered in muddy water, happy as...a pig in mud?

An elephant in mud, he thought, changing the analogy to suit the girl and the time and the place.

It was doing things to him. Standing here, in this almost wilderness, on the edge of nowhere, with the sun on his face, the weathered old farmer beside him, more elephants in the distance, these two elephants in the water before him—and Allie, all cares forgotten, happier than he thought he'd ever seen a woman.

More beautiful than he'd ever seen a woman.

Jack was looking at him sort of quizzically and

he had a feeling the man was seeing more than he wanted him to see. Or was that just because of the weird, exposed way he was feeling?

'She's beautiful,' the old man said, and Matt thought—yes, she is.

Allie was standing again, back on Maisie's back. Maisie was filling her trunk with water and spraying it behind, something they'd obviously done years before and loved. Minnie was beside them, splashing and spraying as well.

But then...

Suddenly the younger elephant tried the same as her mother, filled her trunk with water, lifted it high to spray—but, as she did, she swept her trunk across her mother's back.

Swiping Allie straight down into the water.

No!

She was in the water. She was under the water, and if Matt couldn't see her, neither could the elephants beside her.

She sank straight under with the impact of the fall. Maisie shifted around as though searching for her. The water churned...

And Matt was in there. He was hardly conscious of moving, but one moment he was talking to Jack, the next he was diving hard and deep, straight through the murk, straight to the spot where Allie had fallen.

Somehow he reached her. It was instinct, luck, something, but somehow he had her and hauled her back, away from the animals moving nervously forward. The water was deep and murky and the elephants were shifting in alarm but he had her tight and he wasn't letting go. He hauled her to the surface just as Minnie surged forward.

The elephants could see them now, and they meant no harm. Maisie lurched as if to block off her daughter, and somehow Matt hauled Allie sideways and back towards the bank. Finally he found his feet in the mud and hauled Allie out of the water and out of danger.

What had just happened? A moment's inattention...

He felt his knees sag as he realised how close... how close...

The elephants were now stock still in the water. Jack had surged forward almost as fast as Matt—he was knee-deep in the mud—but he, too, stopped.

Then Maisie took one, two ponderous steps forward and lifted her great trunk and touched Allie's face. She checked her out with her trunk as Matt had seen mother elephants check their babies in wildlife documentaries.

Documentaries. Not real life.

In reality, Allie had fallen and if one of these huge creatures had moved sideways before he'd got there…

He was holding Allie hard against him and he felt her shudder. She didn't flinch from Maisie's touch, though. She stood within the circle of Matt's hold and she touched Maisie's trunk in turn.

'I'm sorry,' she whispered. 'I gave you a fright. I forgot to watch Minnie.' *She was talking to Maisie?*

'It's the way accidents happen,' Jack growled in a voice that said he was as shaken, or more, as they were. 'You forget the power of these guys. They know you, girl, and they're friendly but they're elephants, not toys.'

'Which is why they're here and not in the circus,' Allie managed, but she wasn't moving from Matt's hold. 'I should never… That was so dumb. But it was great.'

'Thanks to your man, here,' Jack said.

'He's not my man.' Her knees were giving in on her, Matt thought. He was holding her up and she needed it. It was okay by him; for now, for this moment, he was her man, whether she willed it or not.

She stood still, taking her time to recover, and Matt was happy to hold her for as long as she needed. Jack stood back and waited as well, and the elephants stood and silently watched, as if they, too, were coming to terms with what had happened. But that was crazy. Anthropomorphism, Matt thought—attributing human traits to animals. It was sentimental nonsense.

But as Matt watched Maisie watch Allie, as he felt Allie's shudders fade, as he stood still while Maisie's trunk explored him in turn, it was impossible not to feel that way.

Maisie's trunk felt like a blessing. Look after my girl.

Thanks to your man, here...

That was how he felt right now. Her man.

Because she felt like his woman.

Nonsense. This was emotion, with no basis in reality.

Except the girl he was holding in his arms felt every inch real, felt every inch a woman, felt every inch a part of him.

His woman.

One dangerous moment had shifted his foundations. He needed to get on firm ground—which involved getting out of this dam.

Before Allie could object, he swung her into his arms and strode out of the muddy water, setting her gently on the bank. He held her for a moment, held her shoulders, then reluctantly let her go.

She didn't move far. She still looked white-faced and shocked.

Emotion be damned, he moved back in again. He put his arm around her shoulders and tugged her against him. Just until she'd recovered, he told himself as they both turned to face Jack.

'You're really okay?' Jack demanded and he was white-faced, too, or as white-faced as a weathered farmer could possibly look.

'I...I'm fine,' Allie said. 'Just paying the price for being dumb. I'm sorry I scared you.' She glanced back towards the elephants, who'd obviously decided things were okay, they could go back to water play. 'What...what happens now?'

'With these guys?' Jack's face turned even more grim. He stared at the great elephants and then he turned and looked into the distance. There were beef cattle grazing peacefully close by, but they could see another three elephants behind them. And two giraffes. 'I'm starting to face it,' he said.

'Myra and I run this place on the smell of an oily rag, but we don't make ends meet. The problem is, these guys live for ever. I started this place when I was wealthy, but I'm not any more. People felt sorry for individual animals—circuses and the like. No one wants to be the one to put them down so they've paid to have them sent here. Five years' keep. Ten years' keep if we're lucky. But Myra and I are getting old. We're running out of steam and we've run out of money. That's why I decided I had to pull in what's owing, only people like you are coming back to me saying sorry, there's no more funding. Myra and I need to retire. My son and his wife would take this on in a heartbeat if it was a business proposition but it's not. We have to walk away.'

He looked across at Maisie and Minnie, still cavorting in the water like two kids instead of a forty-year-old and her eighteen-year-old daughter. 'I'm sorry, lass,' he said. 'But I've made so many enquiries. No one wants them. No one has the room or the facilities to keep them right, and I suspect you'll be with me when I say I'd rather put them down than have them go back to the lifestyle we saved them from.'

'All the animals?' Allie whispered and it was as if all the breath had been sucked out of her.

'All,' he said.

'How many?'

'Ten elephants, two giraffes, four lions, three tigers, four panthers, forty-six monkeys, one gorilla, two bears and seven meerkats.' He managed a smile. 'We might manage to keep the meerkats. Building them an enclosure and keeping them happy might keep me happy in my old age, though I'm not sure how they'll go in a retirement village.'

'They'll be awesome in a retirement village,' Allie said stoutly but she was watching Maisie and Minnie, and Matt could see the iron will needed to keep her face under control. He was holding her and her body was rigid. 'Oh, Jack…there's nothing I can do,' she whispered.

'I know,' the farmer said gently. 'You did what you could as a teenager. They've had ten great years because of you. If it finishes now…' He didn't continue. He didn't have to. 'Do you two want towels? Showers?'

We're fine,' Allie said, starting to recover. 'It's hot. We'll dry. Can you show us the lions?'

So Jack walked them across to the lion enclosure and Matt kept holding her because it seemed the right thing to do. She needed him.

After a scare like that, she'd need anyone with steady legs.

That didn't seem important. What was important was that now she needed *him*.

Allie had fallen silent. Had it been a mistake to bring her here? Matt wondered. Would it break her heart? But even if these animals had to be put down, she'd want to have seen them.

Better to have loved and lost than never to have loved at all...

Where had that saying come from? He didn't know, but suddenly instead of Allie and her elephants—or maybe as well as Allie and her elephants—he was thinking of Margot and her soldier fiancé.

Better to have loved and lost...

Why did it feel as if there was armour there and something was attacking it? It was as if armour was being picked off, piece by piece. There was a big part of him that wanted—needed—to retreat, to regroup, to stop holding Allie, to stop looking at Allie. He was thinking...thinking...

He saw Jack glance at him and then at Allie and

he wondered how much the old man saw. Jack could read animals. Could he read him?

That'd be hard. He could hardly read himself.

The lions were difficult to see. Their enclosure was magnificently built, double fenced, the fence embedded deep into the ground so nothing could dig through. It must have cost a fortune, Matt thought, as he saw it stretch away beyond their sight. The ground beyond was undulating, with trees and rocky outcrops, natural shelter, another waterhole. It was as close as Jack could make, Matt thought, to the wilds these creatures belonged in.

Jack handed Allie field glasses and pointed to a group far to the left. 'Yours'll be the old man,' he told her. 'Prince is still magnificent and Hilda's loyal to him. Zelda died of natural causes last year. The other three in that pride are all lionesses from a guy's private zoo. He made money in the IT boom, set up a private zoo, but his firm went bust so now...' He shrugged. 'Ah, well. I've done the best I can for as long as I can, but it's over.'

Enough.

All the time he'd been talking, walking, watching, no matter that his emotions were in unaccustomed overdrive, Matt's banker brain had been working. Yeah, he'd been distracted by Allie—who wouldn't be distracted by Allie?—but somehow he now reverted. Focus, he told himself, and he did.

'You say your son would take over here?' he asked Jack. 'If it was a viable business?'

'Yes, but it's not,' Jack said shortly.

'Do you and Myra want to go live in a retirement home—with or without meerkats?'

'There's no choice. The house is falling down. All we have goes into these animals. Myra has arthritis. She needs...'

'Help,' Matt said softly. 'Major help. Would you mind if I looked at your books?'

'There's nothing to see,' Jack said bleakly. 'Outgoings equals incomings multiplied by three.'

'But I can't see a scrap of waste,' Matt said. 'I can't see a hint of mismanagement. You know, Bond's Bank has a vast international reputation. As part of our business model we take on projects that do our corporate image good. Usually they're big and visible and attached to major charities, but this...' He stood and gazed around him, at the vast outback landholding, at the elephants in the distance, at the lions in the foreground. 'There'd be more animals than these needing homes,' he said, and it wasn't a question.

'Every week I get requests,' Jack said heavily. 'I can't take them, and I know they get put down.'

'Allie, your camels could come here. They'd like it here.'

'Camels,' Jack said, and brightened. 'That'd give me stuff to learn about.' But the brightness faded. 'You're talking fairy tales, son,' he said. 'Do you have any idea how much this place is losing?'

'I suspect I do,' Matt said absently. 'And I have a board I'd need to bulldoze. Would you have any objection to the Bond logo going on your website?'

'What website?'

'The website Bonds Public Relations team would build for you.'

'But...'

'We don't do things in halves,' Matt went on, working on his theme. Still not looking at Allie. This was business, he told himself. This was nothing to do with a soaking, bedraggled woman who was looking at him with the beginnings of hope in her eyes. 'If we decide to put our fingers in this pie...' He hesitated. 'It wouldn't be a finger. It'd be a whole fist. Or an arm right up to the chest.'

He glanced across at the decrepit homestead. An elderly lady was standing on the veranda, watching them, shielding her face from the sun. With a flash of intuition, he thought—that's Mrya and she doesn't want to be here because she thinks we're talking about putting these animals down.

'We'd build two houses,' Matt said. 'One for your son and one for you. No, make that three. Let's put in a manager's residence as well so your son can take a break when he needs to. You run beef cattle, to make a living, right? My proposition is that you keep doing that if you wish, but you no longer need to. We'll take on the entire costs of maintaining the sanctuary, including generous wages for all of you. We'll examine how much land you have here, thinking about expanding if we need. If you're knocking animals back…Bond's wouldn't want them knocked back or put down. You'll need more staff and we can organise that. Other banks sponsor sports clubs or car races. I'm thinking Bond's will be in the business of saving animals instead.'

'But…' Allie said, and she'd lost her bluster. Her voice was scarcely a whisper. 'But what we owe… What everyone owes…'

'It'll be retrospective,' Matt said. 'We're taking on these animals as of now but we'll take on the debts as well. Bond's has the resources to pull in debts from those who can afford it but the animals' survival won't depend on repayment. For those who've paid for years, that'll be deemed enough. If you wanted to make this place better for your animals, Jack, where would you start?'

The man looked dazed, as well he might. 'I don't...I don't know,' he managed. 'My son has all sorts of dreams. Myra has all sorts of dreams.'

'I'll have my people contact your people then,' Matt said and grinned and shook his hand. 'This can work for both of us. As a PR exercise it'll be magnificent. By the way, you need a name. Does the farm have one?'

'No,' Jack said faintly. 'We've stayed under the radar. Kept it quiet, like.'

'Then maybe we need to change that. It'll mean more animals come to you; you'll need more resources to handle them, but we can cope with that. We're talking long-term funding.'

The commercial part of him was kicking in now, seeing possibilities. He'd hardly touched the structure of the bank since his grandfather had died. It was a staid institution, insular and secure.

Maybe it was time to break out.

'We need an angle,' he said. 'A name...'

'What about Bond's Unleashed?' Allie said. She'd pulled away from him to use the field glasses but suddenly she was right in front of him, staring up at him with shining eyes. 'Bond's Unleashed, for all of you.'

'Bond's Unleashed...' The words drifted, the possibilities opening. Like the girl before him. Possibilities...

'Letting go,' Jack muttered. He stared around at the animals and he stared back at Matt. 'This'd be me letting go of the responsibility—with your blessed bank taking over.'

'Bonds unleashed all over the place,' Allie said and Matt thought...Matt thought...

Bond's Unleashed. He knew it'd work. He could see it.

But mostly all he could see was Allie.

'You need a great snarly lion on your banking logo,' Allie said and he thought incredulously— this is a businesswoman. She has business smarts.

She's beautiful.

'You could use Prince,' Jack said doubtfully. 'But he's more smug than snarling.'

'If Photoshop can get rid of cellulite it can turn smug to snarly.' Allie's eyes were glimmering with unshed tears and she reached out and took Matt's hands in hers. 'Matt, are you sure?'

'I'm sure.' The way he was feeling, it was all he could do to get his voice to work.

'And your bank can afford it?'

'Yes, it can. A thousandfold if need be.'

'And I can send the camels here?'

'Yes,' he said and he saw a weight slide from her shoulders. Her face lightened and she looked... younger?

The feel of her hands in his...

Bonds unleashed. The way he was feeling...

'We should check on the rest of your animals,' he said quickly before his thoughts could take him one inch further into territory he was struggling to understand. 'The monkeys.'

She nodded. 'I...yes, please. We should.'

'And you need to meet our meerkats,' Jack said. 'They're not nearly as risky as elephants.' He grinned at Matt, a great, wide grin that made him seem twenty years younger. 'They're playful. You want to play?'

'I'm a banker,' he said. 'I finance this operation; I don't play.'

'You could be unleashed as well,' Allie said softly, and suddenly things seemed right out of control.

'No.'

'No?'

'No,' he repeated and, whether he meant it or

not, the words came out explosively. 'Jack, I'll need a rough idea of what you need to keep this place running until we can get long-term organisation in place. Can I talk you through it while Allie greets her monkeys?'

'Sure,' Jack said easily. 'Myra has the books. She might also have a cup of tea.' He grinned. 'Maybe a whisky as well?'

'No whisky,' Allie decreed, casting a mischievous glance at Matt. 'One, he's my helicopter pilot and two, he's my ringmaster and he's performing tonight. For now, Matt Bond, that leash stays very firmly on.' Then she tucked her hand in his and chuckled. 'But now I've seen you dive into muddy waters and save me from elephants. Now I know that leash can come off at need.'

Allie checked out her monkeys, who didn't recognise her but they looked gloriously content. Matt checked the books and tried to turn into a banker again.

As he went through the financial figures he understood why Jack was in such financial trouble. He should have folded this place years ago but instead he hadn't compromised one bit. He and Myra were living in poverty but the animals were living in luxury.

Jack and Henry…two old men, following their dreams.

Allie following after.

At least he could save Jack's farm, Matt thought, trying very hard to stay in banker mode as he guided their chopper back to Fort Neptune with a seemingly subdued Allie beside him. The Board might even think it was a good idea—Allie's name was pure brilliance.

But he still couldn't save the circus. No amount of money could make ageing performers young again.

'But it's just us now,' Allie said, almost to herself, but she had headphones and mouthpiece on so he could hear every whisper.

'Just us?'

'With pensions and what I can earn, we can afford a place. It was the thought of paying off that debt that was killing me. And the camels…what was I supposed to do with the camels?' She smiled across at him, a glorious, open smile of sheer gratitude. 'I thought you'd destroyed us, Matt Bond. Instead, you've saved us.'

'We've still foreclosed on the circus.'

'Yes, but that was coming anyway,' she said fairly. 'And it hurts, but it would have hurt whenever it happened.'

'Do you want help finding a place to live?'

'You've done enough for us,' she said gently. 'Matt, back there when I heard you make the offer to Jack, I thought I should refuse. It's charity, but then I realised it's not me you're offering the money to. I talked to Myra while you were going over the books. Do you know how close they were to getting all those animals euthanased? I think you're wonderful, Matt Bond, you and your darling bank.'

'Darling bank...' In all the years he'd worked for Bond's, he'd never once heard his bank described as darling.

'Thank you,' she said, and sniffed and then turned and looked at the scenery below and he thought—she doesn't know what else to say.

Thank you.

He didn't want this woman feeling grateful to him, he thought.

Why?

'We'll get as much out of this as we put in,' he growled, but she didn't turn back to him. He heard her sniff again.

'I'm sure you will,' she managed. 'I'm sure you're

a banker through and through, and this is a very sound business decision. But you're a lovely man, Matt Bond, and you make an awesome ringmaster and I don't even mind if you foreclose on our circus—you are one special person.' And with that she sniffed and subsided.

He focused on the controls for a while.

He was one special person?

He glanced at Allie's averted head and he thought of her cavorting in the muddy waterhole with her elephants and he thought of what she was facing now, her life ahead with a bunch of geriatric circus performers and he thought…he thought…

He thought he wasn't that special person. And he thought more chinks in his carefully built armour were being knocked out every minute.

CHAPTER NINE

HE LANDED ON the foreshore. Joe, the pilot, was there to greet them. 'Successful day?' he asked.

Allie glowed and said, 'Fabulous,' and Matt saw Joe do a double take.

They were both filthy but Allie was the filthiest. She was the one who'd played with elephants, and she'd spent time in the monkey enclosure as well. She'd dried out—the day was so warm her clothes had dried on her—but her hair was tangled, her clothes were smeared with mud and she looked... well, she looked as if she'd just come out of a waterhole filled with elephants. But Matt knew Joe wasn't seeing that. He was seeing the glow, the woman underneath, and suddenly the effort to stay a banker was too much. What was resurfacing was that almost primeval instinct to hold her hard and say, *She's mine.*

Instinct was dumb. Instinct was wrong.

Besides, if she was his, what would he do with her? Marry her? Take her back to Sydney? Give her the life of his mother and his grandmother? Matriarchs, raising the next generation of Banking Mathews while he banked on?

What was he thinking? Allie was a circus performer, in love with elephants and dogs and aged performers and he...his life was the bank. Margot was getting better by the day. He'd promised her two weeks, but after that he'd return to Sydney, he'd get his life back and this time in Fort Neptune would fade to the aberration that it was.

Joe was climbing aboard the chopper, waving farewell. 'You're looking good, sir,' he yelled as the rotor blades threatened to drown out speech. 'I'll report back to work that I've now seen you without a tie. And with a girl who doesn't wear a suit. Wonders will never cease. Expect to hit the front page of Business Weekly,' he yelled and then grinned. 'Only kidding.'

And he was gone, leaving Allie and Matt gazing after him.

The roar of the chopper faded to nothing.

They should go.

Where they were standing had been cleared for chopper landing—for emergency evacuation, for urgent transport, not just choppers of itinerant bankers. It was a spit of land reaching out into the bay, with the circus behind them.

The sea was turquoise-blue, calm and still, with the small waves lapping at the shore the only sound breaking the stillness. The fishing boats were all out. There were only the tenders—small rowing boats—swinging at mooring.

It was a perfect day.

A perfect moment.

Where to take it?

It was Allie who made the decision.

She took his face in her hands and she stood on tiptoe.

'Thank you for today, Matt Bond,' she told him. 'Thank you for my elephants.'

And she kissed him.

They'd kissed before. That kiss was still imprinted on his brain, a sweet, tender moment which, for a guy who'd had few such moments in his life, was one he'd remember.

And want repeated? Maybe he did, because he surely didn't step back now.

But, as a banker, Mathew Bond would accept a kiss from a grateful client—or from a woman who wanted to get closer than he willed—and he'd know what to do with it.

He'd kiss back—lightly. He'd take the woman's shoulders—whoever the woman happened to be—and set her back and smile at her. And he had just the right smile.

It was a smile that said the barricades were up. Very nice kiss, thank you, let's move on.

But this...

This was Allie kissing him, and Mathew Bond the Banker might have every intention in the world of moving on but Mathew Bond the Banker wasn't in charge right now.

This was Matt, the guy underneath all that armour. All day long—or maybe it was since he'd met Allie, something had been chipping away, chipping away. He felt weird, exposed and uncertain.

Or he *had* felt weird, exposed, uncertain. What was surfacing now was something deeper again.

Primeval need.

The need to gather this woman to him and hold.

He'd felt it when Joe had smiled at her and he'd managed to suppress it. He'd been holding back. But now she had his face in her hands, she was right before him, she was on tiptoe, her lips had found his—and she was kissing him.

Hard, fierce, wanting.

This was no kiss of polite thanks. This was not even a kiss of desire for a relationship. It wasn't a kiss of consciousness at all.

It was, quite simply, a kiss of passion.

All day he'd watched her emotions see-sawing. All day he'd seen something he'd never seen before—a woman totally exposed. Her love for those great elephants was deep and real. Her joy in knowing they'd live had unleashed any inhibitions.

But this wasn't a kiss of thanks. It was part of that same raw emotion, and he knew it the moment her lips touched his.

Fire met fire. He took her by the waist and drew her to him, deepening the kiss, and it felt as if their bodies were fusing to become one.

All day the chinks in his armour had been growing wider. Now it was as if the last of the brittle pieces were falling away, leaving him wide open—and this woman was sliding right in.

She was reaching places he hadn't known existed. The warmth of her, the heat, was wrapping itself around his heart, leaving him crazily vulnerable, but he was loving it. He was holding her and that was what he intended doing. Holding. How could he not hold on to this loveliness? How could he step away from this woman?

Gloriously, she was kissing him still. She'd taken his face between her hands and lifted her face to him. She was opening herself to him and the sensation was indescribable.

What was happening to him? It felt as if all his foundations were crumbling to nothing.

But now wasn't the time for wondering about foundations. Who cared for foundations when he was holding her, crushing her breasts against his chest, feeling her mould to him, feeling her hands twine around his head, her fingers in his hair, feeling her mouth open under his, her tongue search as he wanted to search...

Now was simply for being.

Now was for kissing a woman called Allie.

What was she doing?

She was kissing a man who was twisting her heart as it had never been twisted.

He'd saved her elephants. She'd have kissed him if he was King Kong.

But not like this, she thought, dazed. Never like this.

Why was she kissing him?

It was meant to be a thank you, she thought, but she knew that was just an excuse. She'd been aching to kiss him. Aching to touch him.

Why?

Because he was a banker who'd saved her animals?

Because he was one hot guy?

Because he'd saved her today?

None of those things. She was being honest with herself here. She'd been sitting next to him in the chopper for the last hour and she'd been glancing at his face and she'd been thinking...

He's vulnerable.

Poor little rich boy?

But there was no need to take that to extremes, she'd told herself dryly. There wasn't a lot for her to feel sorry about in Matt Bond's world.

And yet as she kissed him now, as she savoured the feel of him, the strength, the heat, the sheer masculinity of this gorgeous hunk of male, that strange feeling was still with her.

He felt...empty, she thought. Alone.

A loner?

The two things were different.

She'd been brought up in a circus family, surrounded by people who loved her.

Did Matt have anyone who loved him apart from Margot?

Did he want anyone else?

She ought to pull away and think about it, but thoughts weren't operating all that efficiently right now.

Her toes were curling.

Her fingers were in his hair. He had the most gorgeous hair, thick and black and curly. He used some sort of product that tamed the curls when he was in his suit, when he was playing the ringmaster, but today had got rid of any product. He was washed and wind-blasted, there was farm dust in his hair, her fingers were tangling...Ooh.

She might or might not love Matt Bond, she decided at last, but she loved his hair.

And, in turn, his fingers were investigating her tangles, gently, slowly, as if exploring every fibre—then drifting downward from the crown to her throat.

His fingers...

He was making love to her with his fingers.

She was having an orgasm here. She was standing out on the spit on Fort Neptune's harbour, she

was being kissed by a man she'd met only days before, the kiss was public property—anyone shop-
ping on the esplanade could see this kiss—and her
insides were melting and this man's hands were
driving her wild and he was just touching her hair
and her throat, for heaven's sake, and she thought,
she thought…

She thought if it was in private she might rip his
clothes off right here. Right now.

Um…it wasn't private. She was kissing a banker
in full view of the world, and she'd instigated the
kiss, and if she didn't stop soon things would get
well out of control, and she'd likely be tarred and
feathered and run out of town as a scarlet woman.

And she'd deserve it.

Right, then.

Somehow she moved—she must have moved—
she must have made some vague motion of pulling away because, appallingly, he responded. He
put his fingers to her lips as if it needed touch to
break the seal. He pulled back, just a little, and the
next moment he was holding her at arm's length
and she was looking into those gorgeous dark eyes
and watching him smile at her and she was thinking….he's just as confused as I am.

And she was drowning in that smile.

'Good…good kissing,' she managed, and he managed a chuckle in return. She wasn't fooled. He was as shaken as she was.

'It's good that we're practising,' he said in a voice that confirmed it. 'We might get good enough to put it on the circus programme if we keep on like we are.'

'We hardly need to put it on the programme.' She glanced across the road, to the shops, to a small cluster of interested onlookers. 'We're giving a free performance.' She shook herself, hauled back from his grasp, fought for reality. 'Speaking of performance…'

'You have heaps of time.'

'Yes, but I need to go visit Grandpa first. I need to tell him what's happening at the farm.'

'You want me to come with you?'

He said it lightly, but it wasn't light. She knew it wasn't light. It was a suggestion that they might take this further.

Girl kisses boy.

Girl takes boy to visit Grandpa.

Not wise. Not wise at all. She gave herself a quick mental shake, reminded herself who she was, where she was, of all the people who depended on her, of how messy a relationship with this guy could be, and about thirty other very good reasons why she should be wise. Regardless, she almost caved in and said yes, but the reasons were there and she was a grown woman and she had to have some sense. Sense for both of them.

'Thank you, no,' she said, struggling to sound light. 'It's time I got back to normality. Thank you for today, Matt. Thank you for what you've done. Thank you for everything, but now I think it's time to move on.'

'That was some kiss.' He'd barely got in the door before Margot was right in front of him, her eyes twinkling with pleasure. 'I didn't know you had it in you.'

'Margot...'

'In front of the whole town,' she continued. 'In my day that'd constitute engagement.'

'Margot!'

'Well, why not? Oh, Matt, she's lovely.'

'She is,' he said tightly and headed for his room. He needed to shower and change—and he needed time to himself—but he was reckoning without Margot.

She was no respecter of persons, his Great-Aunt Margot, and she was no respecter of privacy. He walked into his bedroom and she walked right in after.

'So now what?' she asked.

'I go and play ringmaster at tonight's performance.'

'That's not what I mean.'

'That's all I'm capable of meaning right now,' he told her. 'She's a great girl but I've known her for less than a week—and I can't see her fitting into my world.'

'Your world of banking?'

'What else do you think I mean?'

'Raymond didn't think I'd fit in at Fort Neptune,' she said stolidly. 'I proved him wrong. It's a pity I lost him before I proved it.'

'This is nothing to do with you and Raymond.'

'No, it's all about courage. You keep your emotions filed under P for private, like the rest of your dratted family.'

'Like you, too,' he said, goaded. 'You lost Raymond sixty years ago and you've buried yourself ever since.'

'Living in Fort Neptune is not burying myself.'

'No,' he said shrewdly. There were things he'd thought about his Aunt Margot, things he'd never said, but if she was goading…and if she'd decided to die anyway… 'But what about Duncan?'

'Duncan?'

'You know very well who I'm talking about,' he said. 'The Duncan who stops by every morning to make sure you're okay. The Duncan who's rung me through the years to tell me things he thinks I ought to know—like when you broke your leg on the cliff and didn't think to tell me. The Duncan who rang me and practically bullied me down here because he's so worried—and he told me he asked you to marry him fifty years ago but you refused because you said you never wanted to forget Raymond.'

'He married Edith,' she said stiffly. 'They had a lovely marriage until she died two years ago.'

'So he fell in love,' Matt said softly. 'But he lost and he had the courage to move on.'

'Well, you don't have the courage to fall in love in the first place,' Margot snapped. 'At least I did it once.'

'And it hurt so much you never did it again.'

'So you don't want that hurt?'

'I did hurt,' he said, his voice lowering to match hers. 'I lost my entire family.'

That caught her. She looked up at him, Bond

eyes meeting Bond eyes and he thought—she's almost a reflection of me.

'We're two of a kind,' she whispered, mirroring his thoughts, and he winced.

'Bonds.'

'Cowards?'

'Duncan will be round again tomorrow morning,' he said. 'You jump first.'

'Are you joking? I'm eighty.'

'All the more reason to jump fast.'

'Mathew!'

'I think I'm Matt,' he said softly. 'Some time today I think I left Mathew behind.'

'Oh, my dear,' she said, subsiding, for the anger and aggression had suddenly gone out of her. 'Do you really think that?'

'I don't have a clue. Can you see Allie in my life? Or me in hers? Allie in Sydney or me living in a farmlet with the remnants of Sparkles Circus…?'

'Duncan has ten grandchildren and two Jack Russell terriers,' Margot retorted back at him. 'And I have a cottage I love.'

'So you've decided to die rather than compromise?'

'Compromise is hard,' Margot said. 'As you get older it gets harder. And you…losing your family and finding the courage to start again…I know how hard it is.'

'And I don't even know if she'd have me,' Matt muttered, and Margot's eyes flew wide.

'So you do feel…'

'Of course I feel,' he said explosively. 'I feel and feel and feel and I have not one idea what to do about it. Yes, I'm like you, Margot, but you've spent sixty years thinking about it. I've barely started.'

There was something wrong. He felt it the moment he returned to the circus. Things were underway for the performance, everyone was busy doing what they needed to do, but there was a stiffness, a silence, a tension that he couldn't place.

Allie was preoccupied and silent. 'Nothing's the matter,' she said stiffly in response to his fast enquiry. 'We just need to make this performance as good as it possibly can be, or better. Your bow tie's crooked. See you in the ring.'

The show went on. It was magic, as usual. Allie did a short but wonderful show with her dogs. The camels were back at their best. The tumblers, the magicians, the clowns were all on top of their game, but still there was something…

Previously at the end of each act, the performers

would bounce out of the ring and be greeted with good-natured banter by those in the wings. Now they retreated to silence.

It was as if the volume in the ring was still on normal, but behind the curtain the volume was set to mute.

And the smiles were masks, Matt thought. He did his normal joke routines with Fizz and Fluffy. The clowns hurled themselves into their roles, but underneath the painted clown faces was almost tragedy.

What was going on?

'Are things okay with Henry?' he demanded of Allie in a fast turnaround of equipment where they both had to work together.

'He's fine.'

'Is he still coming home tomorrow?'

'Yes.'

'And Bella?'

'She's fine, too.'

'Then what's the matter?'

'Nothing that hasn't always been the matter,' she told him. 'We're facing facts, that's all.'

He had no time for more.

Finally it was over. Bows were taken, the crowd dispersed and the clearing up started.

This was normally Matt's cue to leave. He'd figured by now that he just got in the way when he tried to help. This was a well oiled machine, and he simply messed up operations.

He didn't leave tonight, though. He'd been watching Allie's face all evening, watching the tension, watching pain. He was starting to know this woman. He was starting to hurt when she hurt.

Was he throwing his heart in the ring?

She wouldn't know what to do with it, he thought grimly. The heart of a Bond? It'd only complicate her life. He'd do what he had to do on the sidelines and then move away—but he had a feeling that there was stuff to be done on the sidelines now.

He headed over to the camel enclosure. Allie wasn't there but she always came here last thing—he knew that by now. The dogs came to greet him. They had the run of the circus and without their sparkly ruffles they were two nondescript Jack Russells, seemingly empathising now with a worried mate.

'You too?' he asked as he sank down on a bench near the camels and both dogs jumped up beside him and put a head on a knee apiece. 'You're worried, too?'

They didn't move, just sat and waited and so did

he, and ten minutes later Allie appeared with a bucket of feed and desolation written all over her.

She stopped when she saw him. He expected the dogs to jump down to greet her but they didn't. He had a weird feeling they were depending on him. *She needs help. Fix it. We're right behind you.*

'You want to tell me?' he said and she stopped short. She stood with the bucket of feed in her hand, as if she didn't know what to do with it. As if she didn't know how to move forward.

She'd shed her sparkles. She was back in her customary jeans and oversized jacket. She'd let her hair out from her performance hairstyle, but residual hairspray was making her curls hang stiffly, at awkward angles.

She'd scrubbed her face free of make-up, but tonight her eyes looked even bigger without the kohl.

Desolate was the only word to describe her.

'Allie…' He rose and lifted the bucket from her hands and set it on the ground. An indignant bray behind him reminded him of priorities. He turned and tipped the bedtime snack into the feed bin, the camels relaxed and he turned back to Allie.

She was still standing where he'd left her. Motionless.

Gutted.

'Allie, tell me,' he said and he couldn't bear it. He moved forward to take her hands, but she did move then. She stepped back in a gesture of pure revulsion.

'It's not your fault,' she whispered but by her expression he could tell she thought it was. 'It had to happen. I…we knew. It was just, I thought we'd have another week before it began. Only of course you have to organise things.'

'Organise what?'

'Carvers rang Grandpa with an offer,' she said dully. 'It's not much. They say we can't even look after our animals. They say they're not paying for our reputation—not when we let wild animals out. Wild—our camels! I'm sure it was Carvers who let them out, using it as a wedge to drive the price down. But Grandpa says what they're offering is all we can expect, so he rang your bank and he accepted. What's worse is that people from Carvers have told every single member of our crew what they thought of them—what their commercial value is. They've offered jobs to five. The rest… well, we all knew it. Anyway, Grandpa got your people here and he signed off on the offer. It's done. We perform for one more week—that's in the offer—but it's finished.'

'Allie...'

'Is that why you took me away today?' she demanded. 'To get me out of the way?'

'No!'

'So your people could come in behind my back?'

Your people...

It would be his people, he thought. The team from Bond's.

Apart from his brief call to organise the chopper, he hadn't been in touch with the bank for days. His foreclosure team back in Sydney would see no need to consult him if Henry received an offer. If Henry was willing to accept, a fast sale to one of the few potential buyers would suit everyone.

It was inevitable, he thought bleakly. It was simply reality hitting home. But now...

Now Matt was the villain of the piece.

Your people.

'Allie, I'm sorry. I didn't know...'

'That you were foreclosing? Of course you did.'

'Yes,' he said. 'I didn't know about today's offer, though. But it does make sense. That's why the team will have moved fast.'

'Your team.'

'Yes,' he admitted. 'I told the team we were giving you two weeks before closing the place down, but we've been putting out feelers for buyers before this.'

'Behind our backs?'

'Henry knew,' he said, firmly and surely. 'It's Henry's circus, Allie. This is not deceit. It's business.'

'Then that's why Carvers will have let the camels out. It's been all over the local papers. Wild beasts from circus roaming town. It's like Carvers wrote the piece. They'll have done it to make sure they get what's left of us for a rock-bottom price. I bet they've been planning it for months. And what they said… They told Fizz and Fluffy they were only fit for geriatric home entertainment—if not inmates. They were triumphant.'

'My people would never have said that.'

'No, but they stood in the background while Carvers said it.'

'I'm so sorry.' He hesitated, but then decided there was no choice but to be honest. 'I've had my phone off, but Allie, if an offer was made, I'd have talked to your grandfather, too, as I'm sure my team has. What they get for the circus goes against your grandfather's debt. It's in all our interests to get a fair price.'

'But to do it so fast... Signing today, and while I was away...'

'Maybe Henry wanted it that way,' he suggested. 'I'm sorry, Allie, but it's your grandfather's decision.'

'I know—' her hands working themselves into fists, clenching and unclenching '—Grandpa has the right. I can't override anything he's done.'

'Would you want it overridden?'

'Done differently. Done...with respect. If I'd known...'

'Allie...'

'Mmm?'

'There is life after this.'

She looked at him, bleak as death. 'Is that what you say to everyone you foreclose on?'

'To be honest, Allie, it seldom happens. We usually do a thorough business appraisal of everyone we lend money to.'

'Unless it's a favour to your Aunt Margot.'

There was a moment's silence. A long moment. More than anything, he wanted to step in to her and take her into his arms. That wouldn't be a usual banker/client gesture of reassurance, he thought, but then Allie wasn't a normal client. With a normal client he could step away.

Her body language said step away anyway.

'They're taking my dogs,' she said, almost conversationally, and he stilled.

The dogs. He glanced behind him and the dogs hadn't moved. They were lying on the bench but there was nothing relaxed about the way they were lying. They were looking straight at him.

Mathew Bond the Villain?

'Grandpa listed all the animals in the asset sheet,' she told him. 'Well, of course he did. They're half the reason people come to see us.' She took a deep breath and stared, not at the dogs, not at Matt, but at the ground. 'People from Carvers have been in the audience for the past few nights. They know what these guys can do. They know they're worth their weight in gold and Grandpa's signed them over. He didn't realise, but it's too late now. All our assets… All our animals. The camels. The ponies. And…and the dogs.'

He stared behind him at the two nondescript Jack Russells. They were circus dogs, but they were also dogs who were loved as pets. He looked at the girl before him and he thought…her heart's breaking.

He moved. Whether she wanted it or not, suddenly he was holding her. He drew her against him, he held her tight, and he felt her body heave with silent sobs. She cried, but not in the sodden sense of the word. It was as if her body had gone into spasm.

A breaking heart? It wasn't an overstatement.

The dogs... The animals... The contract...

How could he solve this one?

Maybe he couldn't. If he knew his team, this sale would be watertight. They'd have brought lawyers. Henry was in hospital so they'd have requested certification of competency before Henry signed. Henry would have signed with as many witnesses as were needed to make things unbreakable.

He thought suddenly of the camera in the audience, and he thought Carvers must have worked on this.

What were you thinking? he demanded of the absent Henry. And then he wondered why he hadn't handled this himself. It wouldn't have happened if he hadn't extended the foreclosure time, if he'd handled the stripping of the circus himself last week.

Or would it? Could he have sensed how much her animals meant to this woman?

And now? All he could do was hold her and wait for the shudders to subside, for her to pull herself together and remember she hated him.

She did pull herself together—sort of—but when she finally pulled away, he didn't see hate. He didn't see anger.

All he saw was defeat.

'I'll talk to them,' he said. 'See if we can organise an exclusion.'

'Are you kidding? They know the dogs are our biggest draw card. Besides, old man Carver hates Grandpa with a vengeance. Two circuses, vying for the same crowds for generations. You have no idea how much Carver will have delighted in today.'

'Dogs shouldn't be for sale. None of the animals should be.'

'They are and they've been sold.' She gathered herself, clicked her fingers and her dogs were instantly by her side. 'The only way we could get out of it is if they won't work. Carvers would never keep them then, but I've trained them to work for anyone. They're wonderful, and now we're paying the price.'

'Allie…'

'Enough. Matt, I need to say thank you. Thank you for your extraordinary generosity towards Jack's waifs and strays. And…and thank you for your very nice kiss. It was…appreciated. Matt, the crew's decided that we'll stick it out for the next week. We won't go out on a whimper, but Grandpa's home tomorrow and if he's home it'll be his last week as ringmaster. We don't need you any more. So thank you, but now it's time for you to go back to being a banker, and for us...for the crew to have our last week being together and then move on.'

He left. She watched him until he was a faint, far off figure in the moonlight.

She slumped onto the bench and her dogs draped themselves over her knees and she thought...

No. She didn't think.

Her world was ending. Her circus was sold. It was the end of life as she knew it.

So why should the hardest part of the night be watching one banker walk along the beach away from her?

CHAPTER TEN

FOR THE NEXT week there wasn't a lot to do, except go back to his original plan when he'd come to Fort Neptune. Make Margot live.

But it seemed Margot had made that decision all by herself, for she didn't have time to die while she was angry.

'I don't understand why you can't buy the circus outright,' she snapped at him. 'You have enough money…'

'I should have bought it,' he conceded. 'But it's too late now.' The sale had gone through so fast he hadn't seen the connotations. Sparkles was no longer a viable business, but for Allie to lose everything…

She hadn't lost everything, he reminded himself. Henry's debts were sorted. Allie and her grandparents could move on, debt-free. Allie would have no further financial commitment.

But she'd have emotional commitment as far as the eye could see. She was still committed to living with her grandparents and great-uncles and she was losing her dogs. The camels and ponies were bad enough, but the dogs?

There was nothing he could do. The contract was watertight. All they could hope for was that somehow the animals proved unsatisfactory and were discarded.

How unlikely was that?

'It's breaking your heart, isn't it?' Margot said and he realised he'd been staring into the dregs of his breakfast coffee for the last five minutes. 'So do something.'

He'd tried to. He'd rung the head of Carvers and offered to buy the animals back, no matter what the price.

Ron Carver had simply laughed.

'I've watched that damned little circus take the best spots, the best crowds, ever since I took over this business. Forty years of watching, and now it's giving me pleasure to rip the guts out of it. Nothing's for sale except what I discard. I'll let you know when I'm in the mood for deciding what's rubbish and what's not.'

Rubbish. The detritus of Sparkles Circus. The detritus of Allie's life.

He was being melodramatic, he thought grimly.

Sparkles was a business and businesses closed down all the time. People moved on.

Allie would move on.

So what made his gut clench every time he thought of her?

'I'll take you to the circus this afternoon,' he told Margot.

'Duncan's taking me,' she said, and he nearly fell over. Duncan, town mayor, long-time friend, had been excluded from Margot's life for months. Last night Matt had arrived back at Margot's cottage to find Duncan and his dogs just leaving. Duncan had given him a sheepish grin and he'd thought— whoa…

Stupidly, he'd also had a very adolescent thought. *Margot doesn't need me either.*

He was used to being a loner. What was wrong with him?

Duncan was taking Margot to the circus? How big a statement was that?

'Maybe I shouldn't go, then,' he said slowly. 'It's time I backed away.'

'Oh, for heaven's sake… It might be time Bond's Bank moved away,' she snapped. 'But not us. We have a week left of Sparkles and I'm making the most of it. And you… Your bank has done what it had to do, so now you can close the door on your business dealings and be a friend. Or more. Don't tell me you're not personally involved. You kissed her in front of the entire town. You've fallen hard.'

'I haven't.'

'If you can't admit that to yourself then you're a fool, and one thing I never thought to think was that my nephew was a fool. Help me get ready. We're going to the circus.'

The circus was supposed to be sold out but somehow Margot and Duncan ended up where Margot always sat, in prime position. Matt, however, had no intention of sitting where he could be seen.

Fizz saw his problem, though. 'It might be your bank but this isn't your fault, mate. Allie's told us what you've done for the old animals. Come and stand in the wings. There's a spot where Allie won't be aware of you.'

How did Fizz know he'd rather stay out of Allie's sight? He hardly knew himself, but he stood in the wings that afternoon, that night, the next day...

He watched Henry play his time out as ringmaster. He watched Fizz and Fluff play with their cannon for the final times. He watched Tinkerbelle and Fairy turn themselves inside out for their mistress and quiver their delight.

He watched Valentino catch Miss Mischka, he heard the crowd gasp in wonder and he thought—don't drop her. And then he thought—she's falling anyway. What would her life be away from here?

He cared so much.

He watched on and, the more he watched, the more he knew the armour he'd so carefully built around him was shattered. He'd built the armour to avoid pain but the pain was here with him regardless. It was as if Allie was a part of him, something he hadn't known was missing but now he was achingly aware of its loss.

How could he lose what he'd never had?

How could he move forward from here without his armour? he thought desperately. How could he possibly persuade her to let their two worlds collide?

A banker and a girl in pink spangles.

He had to try.

She knew he was watching her and her heart twisted and twisted. Pain was everywhere.

She wanted him to go away.

No. She didn't. The last thing she wanted was for him to leave, but it had to happen.

Her life was the remnants of this circus and she was committed for as far as the eye could see and further. He was heading back to Sydney. She was headed to a ramshackle farm and poverty and caring.

She wouldn't have it any other way, she told herself fiercely as the week wore on. This was her choice—she chose family.

Matt was a man who walked alone. For a glorious short time she'd let herself fantasise about walking by his side, but that was all it had ever been.

Fantasy.

Friday night. The final performance was the next day. The air of impenetrable gloom was settled hard. Even those who'd been offered new jobs, who were continuing with Carvers, seemed grey. Their performance had been impeccable, but Matt saw the professionalism that masked the sadness.

During the week Duncan had been great, the elderly mayor now Margot's permanent escort, but tonight was his granddaughter's ballet performance. So Matt took Margot home after the circus, settled her with hot cocoa, watched her being sad as well—and then left.

'You're going back to talk to her?' Margot demanded.

'Yes.'

'Make sure you get it right.'

'I don't know if there is a right,' he said heavily. 'But I need to try.'

'Like I'm trying with Duncan,' she said approvingly. 'Good boy.'

The camels' last meal was more a midnight snack. Camels were supposed to be able to go for a week between meals, Allie thought as she fed them, but no one had ever told these guys.

Would Carvers want them? The contract said that Carvers had first rights to all the animals, but if they didn't perform to expectation they'd be returned. Win-win for Carvers, she thought grimly. There'd be no long-term care expenses for animals past their prime for Carvers.

'I'll offer to take you back when you're ready for retirement,' she told them sadly. She thought the ponies would come back—they were getting old and slow. She'd organised space for them in her life plans.

And if the camels were returned? Jack would love caring for them.

Matt would pay.

She'd been aware of him in the wings every performance for the last week. She knew he'd been talking to all the guys except her. Because he'd been ringmaster, albeit briefly, the crew treated him as one of them.

But he wasn't. He was a banker, in the wings, waiting for the curtain to close. She avoided talking to him and he didn't push it.

What was it about Matt that made her feel desolate? More desolate even than losing the circus.

As desolate as losing her dogs? At the end of tomorrow's performance, Carvers would move in and they'd be gone.

They were lying on their customary bench now, watching her scratch Pharaoh's ears, just watching. They knew something was wrong.

She couldn't bear it.

'Allie?'

She didn't jump. It was almost as if she'd expected it—Matt's voice coming from out of the dark.

'I've almost finished,' she said inconsequentially, and stopped scratching Pharaoh and turned to face him.

He was a shadow in the night, dark and lean. He was wearing his gorgeous coat. Even though she could hardly see his eyes, she knew what his expression would be. She knew his eyes would be filled with concern.

All week she'd felt his concern. He was concerned for all the crew, but for her... She felt as if he was ready to scoop her up, lift her from this world, take care of her as he'd taken care of her animals.

'Allie, you can't do this on your own,' he said, and his words confirmed it.

'Do...do what?'

'Margot's friend, Duncan, is the local mayor and his son's the town's realtor. He says the place you've found to live in is basic. Really basic.'

'It's fine.' She'd looked at all the places they could afford to rent, and had found a big old weatherboard house, a mile out of town, with four bedrooms and enough land so if Carvers discarded the ponies...*when* Carvers discarded the ponies...

The dogs.

Don't go there. Think of the house, she decided, not the animals.

Basic pretty much described it, but it'd fit Allie, her grandparents and Fizz and Fluffy. They could afford it—just.

'What will you do out there?' he asked.

'I've already talked to the local accountant. He's offered me bookkeeping work.'

'And the others?'

'They'll figure it out,' she said, a little bit desperately. 'Everyone has to face retirement.'

'It'd be better if you had a place in town.'

'You know we can't afford it.'

'Let me help.'

She stilled. Closed her eyes. Knew what she had to say.

'Long-term care for ageing circus performers as well as circus animals? I don't think so.'

'I can afford…'

'I know you can,' she said. 'But allow us some pride. We need to move forward, Matt, without Bond's Bank.'

'I'm not talking about Bond's Bank,' he said. 'I'm talking about me. And you.'

She didn't answer. She couldn't. She couldn't think of a thing to say.

'Allie, I think,' he said softly into the night, 'that I've fallen in love with you.'

There was an even longer silence at that.

Love.

Matt.

This wasn't how it was supposed to happen, Allie thought at last, when her mind was capable of rebooting. Girl meets rich, kind and sexy hero. Really sexy. Hero rides to girl's rescue. Hero tells girl he loves her.

Girl loves hero back?

And it hit her, standing in the moonlight with her camels at her back and her dogs watching her, that it wasn't all fantasy. It was possible she did love this man. Or it was more than possible.

For how could she not? He was the kind of hero that fairy tales were made of. He was rich and kind and sexy and he'd ridden to her rescue and he was pretty much all-round fabulous.

But it was more than that. She'd known him for almost two weeks. Was that long enough to see behind the façade, to see the vulnerability, the need, the boy behind the man?

Was it long enough to sense that in this man she'd found someone she could spend the rest of her life with?

Maybe in fairy tales, she told herself, for that was where happy ever after occurred. In fantasy land.

In the world where pink sparkles reigned supreme, where there were no feed buckets and mud-spattered boots, where there was no retired circus family, shattered already, and if she walked away...

She couldn't. She knew she couldn't, and so did Matt. She could tell in the stiffness of his body language, by the way he held himself back when she knew—*she knew*—that every inch of him wanted to walk forward and take her into his arms.

She knew it because that was what she wanted. With all her heart.

The fairy tale. The fantasy that was the dream.

'I can wait,' he said even more gently, and something inside was coming apart. Tearing, ripping, the pain was almost unbelievable.

'Don't,' she said. 'You've done enough.'

'This isn't doing anything for you,' he said, and she heard it then, a pain that matched hers. 'This is doing something...asking something for me. Allie, I need you.'

He did move then, but she hardly noticed him moving. One moment she was standing, numb and still and alone, the next she was folded in to him, wrapped in cashmere, feeling his strength, his warmth, his heart.

'We can do this,' he said roughly, harshly. 'If you feel as I do… Do you?'

'I…maybe. Maybe I do.'

'Allie!'

'But there's no use feeling…like I do.' Her voice was scarcely a whisper. 'There's no way we can be together.'

'If you love me…'

'How can I love you? What use is that?'

'We can work things out. Let me help.'

'Do you honestly think Grandpa would let me take any more of your money?'

'If I married you he would.'

And her world stilled again.

Marriage. The ultimate happy ever after.

Maybe. She'd always been dubious of fairy tales and here it was, the ultimate test.

She could let herself stay folded in cashmere—or she could face the truth? Come on, Allie, she told herself harshly. This was time to be a grown-up.

She was still folded against him. She should pull away but there was only so much a girl could do in the face of…what she was facing…and pulling away from this gorgeous coat was not within her capabilities. Pulling away from this man…

She had to. In a moment. Soon. Even Cinders

had her moment of feeling all was right in her world.

Before reality hit—but reality was now.

'You know, I've always been dubious about Cinderella,' she managed and thought—how can I find the words to explain? She must. 'Matt, I don't have anything to offer.'

'You don't need to offer...'

'How would it work? My family needs me. You know they do. There's no way they—we—could live in the city. Would you come here every Saturday, share a ramshackle bedroom and return to your bank on Sunday? It'd wear thin very fast.'

'It might be fun,' he said. 'And you could come to Sydney. We could share.'

'Sharing's being part of each other's lives.' She took a deep breath, trying to work it out for herself.

'Matt, maybe this sounds dumb, but fairy tales don't work. I'm thinking that in that vast, extravagant palace, with her prince out on princely business six days a week—and Margot's told me how hard you work, Matt Bond, so don't even think of denying it—Cinders must have been pretty lonely after her prince swept her off her feet. And me? Yes, I could get a job in Sydney but every moment

I'd be worried about everyone down here. And down here…what would you do? I can't see it.'

She pulled back from him then, meeting his gaze in the darkness, willing him to understand—and knowing that he already did. The bleakness in his face told her he did.

'No,' she said softly. 'Matt, you'll always be our friend…'

'I don't want to be your friend.' It was an explosion in the stillness of the night, and Tinkerbelle—or was it Fairy?—stood up and barked. Not like she meant it, though. Maybe she was as confused as her owner.

'That's it, then,' she said, and somehow she made her voice sound sensible. 'It's time for us to move on. You've been wonderful.'

'I don't want to be wonderful!'

'You can't help yourself,' she said and she even managed to smile. 'You just are. Matt Bond, super-hero. Prince to the rescue. Off you go on your white charger and find yourself some other maiden.'

'Allie…'

'Matt, no.'

And there it was. She'd said it.

He stood and looked at her for a long, long moment. 'I'll figure this out,' he said at last and she smiled again, but her smile was bleak.

'I know the truth about magicians,' she said. 'Magic's not real.'

'I'll figure it.'

'Matt…'

'There will be an answer,' he said, and he took her hands again, holding her hard, his grip warm and strong and sure.

'And pigs will fly,' she whispered. 'Matt, don't.'

'Anything's possible in a circus. I *will* find an answer.' He tugged her close and she shouldn't let him, she shouldn't, but how could a girl not? She let him. She even tilted her face. She even stood on tiptoe in her disgusting boots so she could meet him face to face.

So his mouth could claim hers.

And she even surrendered. She let herself melt into his kiss. Her arms came round and held him. He held her close, closer, closer. She kissed and she kissed and she kissed and for one last, glorious moment—or maybe longer than a moment—maybe much longer—she let herself believe in the fairy tale.

She kissed her prince and he kissed her back. She loved him with all her heart, with everything she possessed, and then, when the kiss had to end, as even the most wonderful, magical kisses must end, she made herself stand back, look at him one last time and step away.

The fairy tale was ended.

He walked home along the beach. The night was almost moonless. The only sound was the faint lapping of the waves. There was nothing to intrude on his thoughts.

His thoughts should be bleak as death. They weren't.

Would Allie's superhero disappear into the ether without a trace?

He would if he thought there wasn't any hope, but things had changed.

One little word. *Maybe.* Maybe she loved him, and the way she'd said it…

She did, he knew she did, so it only needed…

A miracle?

'Superhero stuff,' he said into the silence. 'Where would a superhero start?'

Find the nearest telephone booth to change into Lycra? Lift her up and carry her bodily back to his lair?

Did Superman have a lair?

How about James Bond?

Forget the superhero, he told himself, and forget the fairy tale. Allie had rightly rejected it out of hand.

His thoughts took off on a different tangent.

He didn't mind the superhero analogy but he agreed it was a one-sided equation. Allie had rejected the notion of hero on white charger and he got it. Equality. Superhero needs superheroine.

He couldn't take her with him. She needed her own lair.

A lair to share?

This was ridiculous, but his thoughts were in free flight.

Go back to basics, he told himself. Go back to what he knew. When faced with a dilemma, he encouraged his employees to brainstorm. Now he was doing it all by himself.

What were the problems? Face this logically. Lay everything on the table and look at every last piece of the equation to see what unbending factor would be bent.

One geriatric circus crew who Allie regarded as family. The odd geriatric animal as Carvers rejected them.

One dilapidated circus.

One Allie who'd learned to be a bookkeeper but looked magnificent in sparkles.

One banker who was solidly based in Sydney, with occasional forays overseas. Who only knew life as a banker.

Margot. He threw her into the mix for good measure.

Camels, ponies, dogs.

Dogs...

That was Priority One of the puzzle, he thought grimly. He needed to find some way to get her dogs back.

But Carver was enjoying this power. It was a triumph, taking the Sparkles' showstopper as well as Sparkles.

An alternative?

Buy Allie a puppy? After all, one Jack Russell was very like another.

Yeah, right. There spoke a man who'd never owned a dog. As if Allie would think that.

Yeah, right... And there went the tangent again.

He'd stopped and was staring out to sea.

One dog was very like another.

One showground was very like another.

One town was very like another.

Unless you knew them. Unless...

He was thinking further. He was looking at every single thing on the table. A girl who lived and dreamed circus. A banker.

A jumble that surely must fit into some sort of order.

It was as if a jigsaw was being thrown up and landing in another frame.

Another picture.

Dogs. Dogs first.

He turned and started striding up the beach, then striding wouldn't do it. He had a contract to pull apart.

He had a girl to win.

He had a magician's hat to pull on.

Striding wouldn't do it. He started to run.

CHAPTER ELEVEN

ONE MONTH LATER, and her life was transformed.

She'd done it. She had all her ducks in a row.

They had the farmhouse almost liveable. For the first couple of weeks Fizz and Fluffy and Bella and Henry had looked grey. The caravans had gone, bought as part of the Carver package, and their belongings had simply been dumped in the sheds here.

It had taken Allie weeks of bossing, of being determinedly cheerful, of threatening and cajoling, but finally they'd all stirred and sighed and decided they might as well get on with it. The house was coming together.

Bella even thought she might start a garden—which was excellent, Allie thought, as once the house was sorted she didn't actually know what everyone was going to do.

Except her. She was going to work and coming home. Her new job was eight until five, Monday to Friday, coping with the basic accounting of five

Fort Neptune businesses—the supermarket, two filling stations, the butcher and the funeral home.

It was so boring that after four weeks she was starting to look longingly at the funeral home.

Today was Friday. Five-thirty. She was heading home for the weekend.

Home. The new normal. Grey. No matter how much bounce she put on for the rest of the household, all she saw was grey.

She could stop in and say hi to Margot, she thought, but Margot was doing okay. Every time she went past Margot's cottage she saw Duncan's car outside or Duncan and his dogs going in and out. His dogs were Jack Russells. She couldn't look at them.

And, worse, Margot looked a little like Matt, and every time she thought about Matt she felt sickeningly sad.

Her dogs.

Her circus.

Matt.

There was a great hole where her heart should be.

Get over it, she told herself. Move on. It's not as if it's a real tragedy. Just pin that dratted smile back on and...

And stop.

She did. Her foot eased off the accelerator.

She'd turned into the farmhouse gate and there was a line-up on the veranda.

Fizz and Fluffy.

Bella and Henry.

Margot and…Duncan?

And Matt.

Matt.

And Duncan's dogs. Jack Russells. Two…

No, three.

Four?

She pulled up and everyone was beaming. Even the dogs.

Matt was beaming.

He had two dogs under his arms.

Duncan had two dogs under his arms.

Matt set his dogs down. The dogs Duncan held wouldn't be set. They were trying to lick Duncan to death.

The two Matt had been holding quivered, stared down at her as if they couldn't be sure—and then they were racing across to her, two balls of canine joy, flipping somersaults, delirious with happiness, and she was down on the ground ruining her prim bookkeeping uniform, trying to hold every inch of them.

And look at Matt at the same time.

He didn't have his coat on. He was wearing jeans and faded pullover. He looked…He looked…

He looked like Matt. She hugged her dogs and she thought she could never love anything as much in the whole world as she loved these two. But Matt was smiling at her and she knew she was wrong.

'We have our dogs back,' Henry boomed unnecessarily from the veranda, and she tried to surface from the dogs enough to ask questions. 'Plus our ponies. Plus our camels.'

'H… How?

'Carver brought them, of course,' Henry said. 'Or his henchmen did. Drove up and practically threw them out of the trailers. Said they were useless, and if the contract hadn't stipulated they be returned to us rather than be put down, that's where they'd be.'

'I've been having them watched,' Matt said mildly. 'We always expected the ponies and camels to be returned; Carvers didn't need them, but the dogs were a different matter. It worked out as we hoped, but I've had undercover security watching over them all the same. Until Carver cracked and tossed them back at us.'

'But… But…' She didn't have the questions to ask.

'Well you may "But",' Duncan said ponderously. 'Too right you had them watched, young man. Of all the risks… If Margot hadn't said she'd consider marrying me if I did it, I'd never have agreed. It wasn't your dogs at risk, miss.'

'They were Duncan's,' Margot said and beamed and somehow, between the dogs, she tucked her arm into Duncan's. 'Wasn't that brave of him? And noble.'

'Very noble,' Allie said faintly and then as the dogs jumped around her feet, she stooped again to hug them. 'No. How can it be noble when I don't understand?'

'Sleight of hand,' her grandfather said and chuckled. 'A feat to be proud of. Your young man is quite a magician. Even I suspected nothing. Fizz did, but apparently Matt thought if he told us all we might give it away.'

'Give…give what away?'

'That last night.' It was Fizz, the old clown, beaming wider even than the painted face he'd worn for so long. 'When the dogs finished in the ring it was me who took them back to your van. That night Carver's men were waiting, collecting everything, but somehow, in the shadows of the wings, two dogs turned into two different dogs.'

'You remember when you got them?' Margot said. 'You bought these two in Fort Neptune. Duncan's two girls are their half sisters. Only they're stupid.'

'Hey!' said Duncan.

'Nice but…placid,' Margot said and smiled. 'And identical to yours. So Duncan took your two girls home, and no one suspected anything. Matt put a discreet watch on all the animals— if there'd been any bad treatment Matt's watchers would have been there in an instant—and when Carver's handlers couldn't do anything with them except make them beg for food, finally he sent them back. It's taken a month. We're sorry it's taken so long, dear.'

'It has, though,' Matt said softly, smiling down at her, 'given me time to put a few more variations to the contract in place.'

'You know,' Margot said thoughtfully, 'if I were you, Matt Bond, and I'm not, so I can't give you advice, but it seems you've been giving me lots of advice lately so maybe you could take a little… If

I were you and a girl was looking at me like Allie's looking at you…maybe you could take her somewhere else and tell her the rest. Somewhere six people and four dogs aren't listening.'

But Allie had something to do first. She was up on the veranda and she was hugging Duncan—or she was hugging as much of him and his dogs as she could.

By the time Duncan emerged from her embrace he was laughing, flustered, and Matt was right beside her, ready to take over the hugging, ready to take Margot's advice.

'I have this really comfy car,' he told her. 'There's room for two dogs on the back seat.'

'But…' She was having trouble breathing. 'What are you going to tell me?'

'I'm not going to tell you anything,' he said. 'I'm going to ask you. Isn't that how it's done?'

'It was in my day,' Duncan said and the elderly town mayor looked at Margot and chortled. 'And my day's still right here.'

He drove her back to town. She was silent for the ten-minute drive. She should ask…but she wasn't brave enough.

She'd sent this guy away. She'd said what was between them was impossible.

It still was impossible, but for now, with her two dogs draped over her knee—yes, they should be in the back seat but discipline had been a bit slack at Duncan's and they approved of being lapdogs—it seemed anything was possible.

For this moment she could pretend that anything was possible.

She hugged her dogs and stared straight ahead and waited for them to reach the beach, but, instead of going to the car park that led to the sand, Matt turned off just before, to the spit of land on the foreshore, to the site of Sparkles Circus.

To the ex-site of Sparkles Circus. Now there was nothing but bare headland. The circus was over.

She climbed from the car and looked at the empty site, at the grass already starting to regrow, at her favourite circus site in the world.

Next year Carvers Circus would play here.

'Next year Carvers Circus can't play here,' Matt said as he came around the car to stand beside her. 'There's been a hiccup.'

'A hiccup.' She was past being astonished.

No, she wasn't. She was pretty much totally astonished.

'Health and Safety issues,' Matt said mournfully. 'Have you noticed how narrow the neck of the spit is? Twenty yards at high tide, and once the circus is out here, there's no other evacuation route, other than by boat. And Carvers Circus is twice the size of Sparkles. Duncan's the mayor. I can't believe he hasn't seen the dangers before this. It only took a nudge, however, and he moved. A man of action, is our Duncan.' He grinned. 'Especially after our watchdog officer showed him a picture of *his* dogs in cages. Next year the circus site will be on the football ground.'

'But the football ground's on the other side of town,' Allie managed, trying to get her head around this. 'You won't get the crowds there.'

'Ah. We knew you were a businesswoman,' Matt said smoothly. 'That's what Duncan's counting on. Fort Neptune has a reputation for keeping its holidaymakers happy. No Sparkles, no happy tourists. So, as any good mayor would, Duncan approached our bank for a business plan to take the town forward. And now we have one.'

'Which would be what?' She'd finally got her breath back. She was still astonished but she was able to look at this guy with suspicion. His eyes were dancing. He looked... Machiavellian.

He looked like Matt, but she was ordering her hormones—desperately—to get over that.

'We propose to turn the spit into a permanent amusement site,' Matt told her, as if he didn't even sense her inner turmoil. 'Funded by the Council, sponsored by Bond's. It'll spread out onto the esplanade, so safety's not an issue. It'll consist of a permanent nautical market, heritage-based, things bought and sold as they would have been bought and sold a hundred years ago. We've asked Margot if she'll take over the organisation and she's already in Bossy R Us mode. Everyone we've talked to is enthusiastic but we need a centrepiece. A showpiece at its heart. Something like an old-fashioned circus.'

'Matt...'

'We see it as a permanent attraction,' he said, and the twinkle had gone now. He sounded deadly serious—banker spelling out business proposition. 'It'd be small, cosy, family-oriented, and it wouldn't have to be spectacular. We see it—Henry, Bella, Duncan and I...'

'Grandpa knows about this?'

'We have talked,' he admitted. 'We had to do something while you did all the town's taxes. Can I go on?'

'I...yes.' Her voice came out a squeak and he grinned.

'Right. Business modelling. Three shows a week maybe, but with added extras. We've talked to the local schools. They'll bring the kids and use it as part of the curriculum. They hope you might be able to teach kids basic circus tricks, so they can treat this as a permanent, loved part of the town. And more. Duncan's talked to the mums' groups, the nursing home, the kindergarten. Everyone wants to be involved. Everyone wants to learn. Allie, Carvers will still come to Fort Neptune, as they have the right to come, and they'll probably still get their audience—people have cars—but they only have the right to be here for two weeks of the year and you're here for ever.'

'Me?' she said blankly.

'That's if you'd like to be a ringmaster,' he said softly. 'Instead of a bookkeeper. For Henry's not going to be able to do it for ever. Though with the show I'm envisaging, age old doesn't matter. We'll just lower the trapeze.'

'I don't...I don't...'

'The bank would finance new equipment,' he said, hurriedly now as if he was afraid she'd think of objections before he could get it all out. 'We'd provide a new big top, new equipment, everything you need. And you have a team. Our dog-watcher reports that even those who were offered jobs with Carvers are already unhappy. You can choose who you want.' Then he hesitated, seeing her confusion. 'But we're not forcing you, Allie. This is something the town needs. Duncan and Margot and I are setting it up, and if Sparkles doesn't want to take up our offer we'll put it out to tender. Carver might even be interested.'

And that hauled her out of open-mouthed, gold-fish-goggle mode like nothing else could.

A tiny circus. A permanent site. A job for the crew as long as they wanted it.

A home.

She saw it. Take away the high risk acts, she thought. Increase the acts that everyone loved, that everyone waited to see, year after year.

Tell Fizz and Fluffy to increase their jokes.

Shine up the cannon.

'Don't you dare offer it to Carver,' she managed. 'If it's okay with you, I think we might negotiate a deal.'

'Consider it negotiated.' He hesitated. 'Only there is a stipulation.'

'Which…which is?' They were standing on the

wide grassy site of circuses past. Behind them was the tiny fort town. Before them was the sea. The breeze was warm and full of salt. The town's fishing fleet was swinging on moorings in the bay as the setting sun played over them.

A plover and his mate were calling to each other somewhere in the grass behind them. Apart from that, there was nothing, nothing and nothing, but a man and a woman with their whole lives stretched out before them.

'I'm the financier of this project,' Matt said, his voice becoming gentle, unsure, as if this last part of the plan was the most likely to be rejected. 'As as financier, I need a hands-on role. You'd have to hand the bookkeeping to me.'

'I'm a bookkeeper.'

'Yes, but the circus you book-kept went bust,' he said, sounding stern. 'How could Bond's possibly finance a venture with such a record unless they took a personal interest? A very personal interest.'

'Which…which would be?' He was so big, she thought inconsequentially. He was so…male. He was Matt.

Mathew Bond of Bond's Bank.

No. Just Matt. A guy with a proposition to take her breath away, with a body to take her breath away, but, at the core, still that hint of uncertainty, as if he, too, was being asked to take a step into the unknown.

'I'd need to live in Fort Neptune,' he said and her breath was taken away all over again.

'Wh…why?'

He hesitated. Thought about it a little. Fought to get it right.

'You know,' he said slowly, as if he was talking through an idea he was only now coming to terms with, 'ever since I can remember, from the day I was born, it was always assumed I'd be the Chairman of Bond's Bank. With my family holding, I'm the major shareholder. I've been trained since birth to sit in the director's chair, to take control of the day to day running of the bank, to *be* Bond's Bank. It was only when I met you that I thought…why? Do I need to be the Chairman of Bond's Bank? Four weeks ago I stood on the beach and did some brainstorming and put everything on the table. Or on the sand. Just like I've taught my employees to do. I put Chairman of the bank on the sand as well, and suddenly I thought—I don't need to pick it up again.'

'But…Matt, it's what you are.'

'Is it? Why?'

'I…' She couldn't think of an answer. She struggled. 'Because you get to wear gorgeous coats,' she said at last and he grinned, and finally, finally he reached out and took her hands and tugged her to him.

'I have three coats,' he said. 'That's enough for one man for a lifetime, especially as I propose moving aside, keeping a seat on the Board but not staying as operational Head. That means I won't spend half my life in Europe's winter, where cashmere coats are needed to keep me warm. I have a helicopter. I can travel. Jack needs a good financial adviser at the farm and I'd like to be hands-on at Bond's Unleashed. I'd like to revamp Bond's public image, but a lot of that can be done online. So I was sort of hoping…no, make that really hoping, that if I bought a house here, commuting at need but basing myself here in perpetuity, I might have something else…*someone else*…to keep me warm.'

'Matt,' she said again, but this time it was different. It was a breath when she was struggling to breathe. It was almost a prayer.

Matt.

'I love you,' he said and her world stood still.

'Love…'

'I've told you before, Allie. You knocked me back because you didn't fancy playing beggar maid to my King Cophetua. This way it'd be different. We'd share a house, we'd share a life, but it would be sharing. You'd be taking Sparkles over from Henry and your life would be based here. Duncan and I think Sparkles could run at a profit almost immediately. You'd be independent.'

'And you…you'd be independent, too?'

'You're pretty good with marketing,' he told her, caressing her with his eyes. 'I suspect there'll be times, lying in bed late at night or early in the morning, when I say, "Love, what do you think about this?" And I was acting ringmaster for a whole week so I pretty much know about circuses. I'm hoping you might do the same.'

'Bed,' she said faintly, because of all the images his words conjured up, that was the biggie. Lying in bed beside this man. Waking up beside him, over and over, for the rest of her life.

Living here. Running the circus here. Watching Henry and Bella enjoy their retirement. Watching Fizz and Fluffy with their pride restored. Watching Margot decide to live.

And at night, home to bed, home to Matt, home to her love.

'Allie…' And she heard his tension. He was holding her, he was smiling at her, he was promising her the world, a future, love, a home and hearth and him.

And he didn't know. He wasn't sure.

'There'd….there'd be stipulations,' she managed.

'Stipulations?'

'Yes,' she said, and her voice cracked a little but she made herself go on. 'You would need to do banking business. There'd be times you would need to go away.'

'There would be,' he agreed, the tension building.

'Then we'd have to always have an alternative.'

'An alternative?'

'An alternative ringmaster,' she said and she smiled and smiled, her eyes misting with tears, her heart swelling so she thought something down there might burst but she didn't care. 'So that if you need to travel, I get to come with you.'

'Allie!'

'I won't stay in my Cinders kitchen,' she said. 'Or the wings of my circus either, for that matter. And I'd really like a bit of hands on involvement in your life, in your bank if we can swing that and in Jack's sanctuary as well.'

'Yes,' he said, just like that, and she looked at him, she really looked at him, and everything sort of dissolved. Melted. It was as if her past was falling away and there was only this man, this moment, this love.

'I love you,' she whispered, finally, at last. 'Matt, I don't…I don't really care about stipulations.'

'It's important to get it right,' he said gravely. 'This is a very important contract you're entering into and, as a banker, I have to warn you to check the fine details. Allie, will you marry me?'

'Yes.'

His eyes darkened and gleamed and he tugged her tighter.

'Didn't I just warn you?'

'You can warn me all you like,' she said and this time it was Allie doing the tugging. 'But you've offered and I've accepted. I have two dogs who witnessed every word. Contract made, Mathew Bond, and there's no way you're getting out of it now.'

'Matt,' he said, because suddenly it seemed important.

'Matt,' she whispered, lovingly, surely, and she held him and held him, and when he tilted her chin to claim her mouth, as she melted into his arms, as her night dissolved into a mist of love and truth and happiness she thought:

Matt.

Superhero.

Ringmaster.

Love.

It was a strange place to have a wedding reception.

Matt and Allie married in the church at Fort Neptune, the church Margot had decreed would be used for her funeral before she'd decided that this wedding would come first. It was even possible now that baptisms would happen before funerals as well, Margot thought happily, as she watched Matt and Allie take their vows. And there might even be another wedding. Duncan was dining at her cottage every night now and the locals were starting to gossip. She'd promised him she'd consider marrying him and maybe she should. A Bond had to be careful of her reputation if she was to stay living in such a small town, and right now living looked good.

But they weren't in Fort Neptune now. They were at Jack's animal sanctuary. *Bond's Unleashed.*

Duncan was holding her hand as Jack made a speech. Matt and Allie stood side by side in their bridal splendour, smiling and smiling, while Jack spoke about the future, about what Matt and Allie had achieved and what they had before them.

For, after this morning's ceremony, the guests had all been transported to the sanctuary. They'd set up a canopy by the dam. There was a small chance that the elephants might be interested enough to move in on the ceremony, in which case the guests were instructed to grab the trays of food and retreat, but the elephants seemed to know. They stood back, Maisie and Minnie and three more of their now permanent herd, and watched as these strange human creatures did what strange human creatures did.

The formal opening of the fresh and newly funded Bond's Unleashed animal sanctuary had been last week. This place was safe in perpetuity. Allie and Jack, newly elected members of the newly formed board, would see to it.

'It's our life's work,' Matt had said. 'And our children's and our children's children. I was bequeathed a bank and a destiny as a banker. Our children—and not one called Mathew, by the way—can do what they like, but we'll raise them to care.'

'How could they not?' Allie had said, and

Margot, watching the two newlyweds, could only agree.

These two were right. These two were fine. The future stretched before them magically, wonderfully, and on impulse she turned to Duncan.

'I will marry you,' she said. 'As long as I can share your dogs.' And Duncan whooped like a teenager and whirled her right off the ground so Margot felt like a girl again and not like an aged spinster who should watch her dignity.

And from the dance floor, where Jack had spread planks over the grass and dust, where Allie and Matt had been persuaded to dance a bridal waltz, Allie whispered to Matt, 'Look at Margot. Look at Duncan.'

Matt looked and smiled—and then he looked down at his bride and his smile grew wider, more tender, enveloping her in a warmth that would stay with her for the rest of their lives.

'Maybe they've found what we've found,' he said, and he took the first steps of the bridal waltz, holding her close, finding the steps worked automatically because Allie's body in her beautiful white bridal gown simply melted into his, and it was as if one body was dancing. One heart.

'Maybe it's catching,' Allie whispered, holding him tight. 'Matt, I love you so much.'

'I love you so much I'm willing to share,' he said grandly, sweeping her round the makeshift floor while their audience, half of Fort Neptune, all of the circus, so many from Bond's Bank, erupted into applause. 'If you knew how hard it was to get all these people all the way here...'

'Just so they can share,' Allie said, and looked around at the audience, at their friends, at the elephants far in the background, and she held Matt and she thought...sharing.

She'd always shared, she thought, but she'd been isolated in her sharing.

Matt had simply been isolated.

But two islands had suddenly become the mainland, the centre, the base on which the future would grow.

'How many kids?' she asked as Matt reached a corner of the dance floor. He was concentrating on a tricky turn, steering his bride so he didn't take her off the boards, so he didn't lose her to the dust.

Her question, though, almost made him mis-step.

'Kids?' he said. He'd thought about them in the abstract, but...real?

'Kids,' she said happily. 'Kids and dogs and ponies and camels and gran and grandpa and uncles and all of Fort Neptune. You'll never be alone again, my Matt.'

'I'll never want to be,' Matt said and then stooped and whispered into her ear. 'Will you wear sparkles on our wedding night?'

'I surely will,' she said and smiled and smiled. 'As long as you wear your top hat.'

'Just wave your magic wand and decree,' he said grandly. 'Who said circuses are all about illusion? Magic does happen. It's happening here.'

* * * * *

Mills & Boon® Large Print

August 2013

MASTER OF HER VIRTUE
Miranda Lee

THE COST OF HER INNOCENCE
Jacqueline Baird

A TASTE OF THE FORBIDDEN
Carole Mortimer

COUNT VALIERI'S PRISONER
Sara Craven

THE MERCILESS TRAVIS WILDE
Sandra Marton

A GAME WITH ONE WINNER
Lynn Raye Harris

HEIR TO A DESERT LEGACY
Maisey Yates

SPARKS FLY WITH THE BILLIONAIRE
Marion Lennox

A DADDY FOR HER SONS
Raye Morgan

ALONG CAME TWINS...
Rebecca Winters

AN ACCIDENTAL FAMILY
Ami Weaver

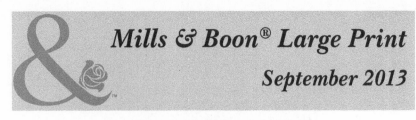

Mills & Boon® Large Print
September 2013

A RICH MAN'S WHIM
Lynne Graham

A PRICE WORTH PAYING?
Trish Morey

A TOUCH OF NOTORIETY
Carole Mortimer

THE SECRET CASELLA BABY
Cathy Williams

MAID FOR MONTERO
Kim Lawrence

CAPTIVE IN HIS CASTLE
Chantelle Shaw

HEIR TO A DARK INHERITANCE
Maisey Yates

ANYTHING BUT VANILLA...
Liz Fielding

A FATHER FOR HER TRIPLETS
Susan Meier

SECOND CHANCE WITH THE REBEL
Cara Colter

FIRST COMES BABY...
Michelle Douglas